Lacey's Story

A Puppy Tale

Also by
W. Bruce Cameron

A PUPPY TALE

Lacey's Story

W. Bruce Cameron

Illustrations by
Richard Cowdrey

STARSCAPE

A Tom Doherty Associates Book
New York

LACEY'S STORY

Copyright © 2022 by W. Bruce Cameron

Reader's guide copyright © 2022 Tor Books

Illustrations © 2022 by Richard Cowdrey

A Starscape Book
Published by Tom Doherty Associates
120 Broadway
New York, NY 10271

www.tor-forge.com

Library of Congress Cataloging-in-Publication Data

Names: Cameron, W. Bruce, author. | Cowdrey, Richard, illustrator.
Title: Lacey's story / W. Bruce Cameron ; illustrations by Richard Cowdrey.
Description: First edition. | New York : Starscape, 2022. |
Series: A puppy tale | "A Tom Doherty Associates Book." |
Identifiers: LCCN 2022016276 (print) | LCCN 2022016277 (ebook) |
ISBN 9781250163400 (hardcover) | ISBN 9781250163424 (ebook)
Subjects: CYAC: Dogs—Fiction. | Animals—Infancy—Fiction. |
Human-animal relationships—Fiction. | Animals with disabilities—Fiction. |
LCGFT: Animal fiction. | Novels.
Classification: LCC PZ10.3.C1466 Lac 2022 (print) |
LCC PZ10.3.C1466 (ebook) | DDC [Fic]—dc23
LC record available at https://lccn.loc.gov/2022016276
LC ebook record available at https://lccn.loc.gov/2022016277

Our books may be purchased in bulk for promotional, educational, or business use.
Please contact your local bookseller or the Macmillan Corporate and Premium
Sales Department at 1-800-221-7945, extension 5442, or by email
at MacmillanSpecialMarkets@macmillan.com.

First Edition: 2022

Printed in the United States of America

0 9 8 7 6 5 4 3 2 1

Dedicated to Betty Bennett,
Bob Clearmountain,
and Marlene Passaro,
who, along with all the talented people at
Apogee Electronics, have done so much
to support my work and success.

Lacey's Story

A Puppy Tale

1

I was having the most wonderful day with Wenling. We were out in the fields where we had spent the morning romping and trying to scare up rabbits. I could smell those rabbits, but they were wisely hiding from me. They know that I am a great hunter dog who has almost caught rabbits many times.

My name is Lacey, and Wenling is my girl. I love her dark hair and how it smells after a day like today, when we have been outside playing. Today she was on her hands and knees digging in the dirt. I could tell she was happy, so I kept running up and jumping on her. A dog needs to do whatever is necessary to make her humans even happier than they already are.

"No, Lacey," she would say with a laugh.

The word *no* has many different meanings. When

it's said with a laugh, it means something like *Let's keep having fun!*

Wenling had carried a box with her out into the fields. She was pulling up stinky grass and throwing it into the box. Soon the inside of that box smelled wonderfully of dirt, but also of something else—something so strong it made my nose crinkle. The odor grew more powerful as she pulled the plants from the earth and tossed them in the box.

"It's such a great time to be harvesting wild onions," Wenling told me. I wagged because she was talking to me, but I hoped she wouldn't throw the plants for me to fetch. Each clump of grass had a sort of ball on the end of it, and I've chased after balls of many kinds. But it was these balls that were giving off that eye-watering odor.

I love a vivid odor as much as any dog. Almost nothing beats the scent of a long-dead animal lying in the sun. Rolling in that kind of bouquet paints my fur with an irresistible smell. Often, though, my girl will pick the very day I have slathered my body with such a perfume to give me a bath, washing away my efforts to smell beautiful. It's such a strange coincidence!

Wenling stood and wiped a hand across her forehead. Then she looked around, beaming "I love living here. Do you love living here, Lacey?"

I heard my name and the joy in her voice, so I wagged.

"I love my friends at school, and I love the fields and going with Dad to the farm. And my favorite place of all is the orchard. We're so lucky to live here!"

I play-bowed, stretching out my front legs long on the ground while my rump stayed up and my tail kept wagging. I was ready to romp or wrestle or even, I supposed, chase the stinky balls—though I couldn't be sure I'd pick them up with my mouth after I ran them down.

"Onions are so sweet in the fall," Wenling told me as she struggled to pick up her now-full box. I trotted happily behind her, and we returned home, crossing fields of long, dry grass. The rabbits remained hidden. They probably didn't come out for a long, long time, because they were so scared of me, Lacey the Rabbit Hunter.

I scampered ahead of Wenling when I smelled home and was at the door whining to be let in as Mom opened it. Mom looks a lot like Wenling, with the same very dark hair and the same smile. Now she gave that smile to both me and my girl.

"What've you got there?" Mom asked.

"Wild onions!" Wenling exclaimed, showing Mom her box. "Don't they smell wonderful?"

Mom looked into the box but hid her disappointment that there was nothing inside but a pile of stinky, dirty balls.

"I'll wash them for you," Mom said.

ZZ came into the room, and we both turned. It was

unusual for him to be home before the sun was lower in the sky, but I trotted up to him agreeably. When it comes to comings and goings, the minds of humans are unknowable to a dog. All we can do is accept people's decisions and have fun in the process.

"Why were you outside looking for onions?" ZZ demanded. "Don't you have homework?"

Wenling frowned. "I do have homework, Father," she replied a bit stiffly, "but it's such a beautiful day." Wenling often calls ZZ *Father*, but everyone else calls him ZZ, and it's just easier for a dog to remember. Sometimes Wenling's word for him is *Dad*, a word other people also sling around carelessly. I long ago decided that *Dad* means "man" the way *dog* means, well, "dog." So someone can say "good dog" to another dog and not be talking about me, even though obviously I am a good dog and they *should* be talking about me.

ZZ nodded. "Yes. I know it's a nice day. I am not telling you that you have to remain indoors. I'm telling you that you could easily take your books to the picnic table in the backyard and study there."

"But, Father—" Wenling started to say.

"No," ZZ responded sternly.

"The onions will make a delicious soup," Mom offered cheerfully.

ZZ scowled. "We discussed this."

"Yes," Wenling replied. I jerked my head to stare at

her because her tone was so sharp. "And I like to grow things. I like to harvest plants. What's wrong with that?"

"What's wrong with that?" ZZ repeated wearily. "I work hard to put a roof over our heads, and I do it by—" He gestured to the box. "By picking things like onions and cucumbers and zucchini. It's hard work, and I'm exhausted when I'm finished. I want more for you, Wenling. You're a smart girl, and you can succeed at anything you put your mind to. I want you to be a doctor or a lawyer—a good career. But you're not going to get there if you get your hands dirty every day."

Wenling folded her arms. "I like getting my hands dirty. I love gardening."

ZZ stared at her. I sensed that he was angry. Maybe he didn't like the stinky balls any more than I did, but he shouldn't have been mad at my girl just because she filled up a box with them. She didn't know any better.

I guess ZZ figured that out, because suddenly his shoulders slumped. "Oh, Wenling. I have not wanted to tell you this, but I'm afraid I can't promise you that we'll be living here much longer. We may have to move."

"*What?*"

I went to my girl and sat in front of her. I could sense her distress and wanted to make her happy again.

"Chase told me today he can't afford to pay me anymore."

Mom gasped, and I looked at her in alarm. Now no one was happy!

"You told us he can't run the farm without you!" Wenling protested.

ZZ shook his head. "No, he can't. His sons are too young."

"I didn't realize it had come to this," Mom murmured. ZZ shrugged.

"I can see if they'll let me have more hours down at the store," Mom said decisively.

Wenling was staring at ZZ. I felt a whimper building in my throat, and she seemed to sense it because she reached down and stroked my head. "Are we really going to have to move?" she asked plaintively. 'When?"

ZZ shrugged again. "I don't know. Even though he can't afford to pay me a salary right now, Chase made me an offer. He said I can be his partner if I want. He'll put it in writing, even, that if the farm ever goes back to making a profit, he'll deed me half ownership."

"Wait, ZZ!" Mom shook her head. "That's so like you, to bury the good news and only talk about the bad. This isn't as if you've been *laid off*. You still have a job, and now you own half the farm."

"Half a *money-losing* farm," he corrected. "Doesn't make any sense to try to claim half of it right now. That would just mean taking on half the debts."

"But still," Mom protested. "The farm has made money before. Times are tight, I know that, but you and Chase are the smartest people in the business. You'll figure something out. It's not like it's the end of the world. You've said it before—farming is a cyclical business."

"Cyclical?" Wenling asked.

"Meaning there are regular cycles," Mom explained. "Sometimes the farm does really well to make up for the tough years. And there's a good balance. The crops from the fields make more money some years, and other years the fruit from the orchard does better."

"Orchard did okay last year," ZZ noted.

"Exactly," Mom agreed with a nod.

"I love the orchard. It's my favorite place in the world," Wenling declared. "We can't move away from the *orchard*."

"I'm not saying we have to move now, Wenling. We'll give it another year or so," ZZ went on. "Also, I talked to my friend Jason—he's going to take me on to close down his restaurant each night, clean up after all the customers have left, lock the doors, take out the trash. I'll make a little money that way."

"Oh, ZZ," Mom moaned. "You already work so hard."

ZZ ignored whatever Mom had just said. He was focused on Wenling. "But I want you to know, Wenling, this is our last try. We can't go on like this much longer."

"Why would we have to *move*?" Wenling asked. She

sounded so unhappy that I felt another whine building up in my throat. "Couldn't you just get a job doing something else? Something here, in town?"

"Wenling," Mom warned.

ZZ sighed. "There's no work for me here. There will be better opportunities in a city farther south. Grand Rapids or Lansing."

Wenling's eyes were wide. "But all my friends are here. My whole life is here!"

"Wenling," Mom interrupted gently. "This isn't just about you. Listen to what your father is saying. Nobody wants to move. We're both going to work hard to try to make sure that it doesn't happen. But if it's what we have to do, it's what we'll do."

"Now do you understand?" ZZ asked gently. "That's why I want you to study. Go to college. Get a good job. So you're never forced to make decisions like this. I've worked that farm since you were born. We had five hands when I started, and now it's just me. But no matter what Chase and I do, it doesn't seem to be good enough. So you will not be a farmer, Wenling. I won't hear of it."

There was a moment of silence, and then ZZ turned and left the room. Soon I could hear running water from the back of the house.

"It's not fair, Mom!" Wenling insisted.

My girl was unhappy. I didn't know why we didn't

go back to her bedroom and lie in bed and cuddle. That always made both of us feel better.

Mom came over and put her hand on Wenling's shoulder. "I know this is hard for you to understand," she told Wenling. "But you'll make new friends wherever we go."

"We've lived here since I was born! I don't want new friends; I want *my* friends."

"I know. But we can't always have what we want, Wenling."

"What about your job, Mom? You can't just quit."

"Well . . . someone always needs retail workers. I won't have any problem finding a new job. And ZZ says the factories in the cities are hiring." Mom shrugged. "He doesn't want to leave any more than you do, honey. It would break his heart to abandon Chase's farm. The two of them are like brothers—that's why Chase wants to give him half the place. But there's only so much we can do. We have no savings, and if ZZ isn't going to make a salary . . ."

"I'll help. I'll get a job!"

Mom's smile was sad. "You're too young to get a job, and anyway, your father would never allow it. He wants you to study, get good grades."

Wenling was still unhappy, so I nosed her hand to let her know she should go back to petting my head. "Yes, so that I can be a doctor or a lawyer. But I don't want that! He doesn't listen to me, and he doesn't understand me."

"Maybe there is a way to combine both things," Mom suggested. "You love farming, and you love to grow things. He wants you to go to college. Perhaps you could get a horticultural degree."

Wenling's sadness was more than I could bear. I threw myself on the floor, sticking my legs up into the air and twisting my back on the carpet, knowing that a happy dog was what my girl needed.

I expected her to giggle and rub my tummy, but she didn't. Mom left the room, and Wenling knelt down to whisper to me. "We can't let this happen, Lacey," she told me solemnly. "I don't want to move. I have to think of something."

I was grateful that her sadness was leaving her. Something else was taking over. It wasn't happiness, exactly, because her mouth was still set in a firm line, but the heartbreak was gone. I sprang to my feet and licked her full in the face.

"Okay! Okay!" she spluttered. "You crazy dog."

2

I was thrilled when Cooper, Grant, and Burke came over to visit, along with their father, Chase.

Cooper is my best dog friend in the world. He is a large, furry white dog with dark patches, and he is strong enough to knock me over when we play. He's always gentle, though, and I can tell from the soft way he nibbles my neck that he loves me as much as I love him.

Both Burke and Grant are friends with Wenling. Burke seems to be the same age as my girl. She spends more time with Burke, which is good because Burke is Cooper's person, and this means I get to spend more time with Cooper.

Grant isn't any dog's person, even though he lives with Burke. I understand this. I live with ZZ and Mom, and they are very dear to me, but I have only one person and that is Wenling.

There are a lot of people without dogs in their lives, which I do *not* understand. There are many dogs, and every single one should have a person, and every person should have a dog. Sometimes dogs can figure out things like this even when humans can't.

Grant is older than Burke and different from his brother in a key way: Burke likes to sit in a chair with wheels. In fact, I have never seen him get up out of that chair except to swim in the pond in the summer. Grant has never once sat in a chair with wheels, in my experience.

I have figured out that Chase is Burke and Grant's father. When people are in the same family, they share a common odor. Long ago, when I lived with my mother dog, I smelled like the puppies who were my brothers and sisters. It's the same thing with people.

Cooper and I knew each other back in those days. We both lived in the same place with our mother dogs, and there were other dogs around, too—lots of them. The same day that Wenling came to get me, Grant and Chase and Burke took Cooper to live with them at the farm.

Back then, as happy as I was to have my own girl, I was upset to think that I would never get to play with Cooper again. But I needn't have worried—Wenling loves me so much that she figured out how I feel about

Cooper. From that day on, she made sure we saw both boys and Cooper a lot. This is one of the many, many reasons I love Wenling so much. She always tries to make me happy.

Both Grant and Burke call Chase a different name: *Dad*. It's because they don't know his name, and so they use that general term. I was proud that I had figured out Chase's real name when these two humans in his own family didn't know it yet.

"Hi, Wenling," Burke greeted. "It's okay, Cooper, you can play. Okay!"

Cooper had been staring hard at Burke until he heard the word *Okay*. It's one of Burke's favorite words, and he uses it a lot.

I like it, too, because whenever Burke says, "Okay!" to Cooper, Cooper starts to play. He happily jumped on my back, and I happily let him. Soon we were running and running around the yard, full of the joy of being dogs together. Cooper tumbled, falling on purpose, so that I could leap on him and mouth his throat with gentle nibbles. In that moment Cooper and I loved each other so much that only our people mattered more. Cooper was my dog, and I was his.

The play felt as if it could go on forever. We both got distracted, though, when ZZ and Chase and Grant unloaded big, long sticks from the back of Chase's truck and laid them out on the ground. What sort of game was this?

The backyard to our house was surrounded by a wooden fence. The gate was always tied shut with a loop of dirty rope. Chase reached out and shook the gate with a gloved hand. "I see what you mean," Chase told ZZ, grinning. "Time to replace this before it falls over."

"A fence is only as strong as its gate," ZZ responded.

The two men and Grant began laying the sticks down on the ground. I would have been satisfied to sit and watch in confusion. Humans do the strangest things! But Cooper was there, so I wanted to play with him instead. A dog has to have priorities.

As we were wrestling, I heard Chase say, "Just got word. It's official: they're shutting down the cider mill."

ZZ grunted in reply.

"Don't know who's going to buy our apples now. I guess we can sell them to the baby food company for a couple of pennies a pound." Chase wiped his face with a gloved hand. "Almost better just to let them rot in the fields."

ZZ's reply to this was to take a hammer and pound on the wood a little bit.

"Dad," Burke ventured tentatively, "remember I asked about the dam they built up at the mill? They already aren't keeping the spillway clear. Who's going to maintain it if they're closed?"

Chase gazed reflectively at Burke. "Now what, again?"

"They dammed up their stream," Burke explained patiently. "But leaves and tree branches blow into the pond and clog up the spillway. So the water keeps rising, especially in the rainy season. If it rises to the top of the dam, it could collapse, and all the water would flow downhill. It could wipe out our house!"

Chase smiled fondly. "You're going to be an engineer someday, Burke. I just know it."

"Wait," Grant objected, "don't you need brains to be an engineer?"

"The dam's a problem," Burke insisted.

"I'll make a call," Chase responded absently.

I ran over to one of the thinner sticks that they were playing with and picked it up and tried to run off with it. Wenling laughed at me.

"No!" ZZ scolded. I dropped the stick. In this case, the word *no* is very close to *bad dog*. And *bad dog* is the worst thing a human can say.

"Lacey is not very well behaved," ZZ observed, pointing his hammer at me. Embarrassed, I seized Cooper's cheek with my teeth.

I felt Wenling stiffen, and I stopped chewing on Cooper's face to look her way.

"Anyway," Chase continued, "the good news is that we've got an offer from a guy who will take the trees off our hands. I guess he grinds them up for wood chips to sell to folks to use them in smokers."

"Chop down the trees?" Wenling gasped. "All of them?"

Both men stared at her as if surprised by her reaction. I stared at her, too, because I could tell she was suddenly unhappy. But we were outside with friends and we had sticks to play with, so what could be bothering her?

"I know, I hate to," Chase agreed, "but he's offering twelve hundred dollars. Since we can't make a profit on the fruit, might as well get some money from the trees themselves."

Wenling shook her head wildly. "You can't do that!"

"Wenling," ZZ said sternly, frowning. "This is not your business."

Burke spoke up. "Hey, let's take the dogs, go for a walk."

Wenling bit her lip.

"Cooper, Come."

And just like that, Cooper was done playing with me. He raced to Burke's side, so I went to Wenling's.

"You got this, Dad?" Burke asked. "Or do you need me to stay and supervise Grant?"

Grant rolled his eyes, and Chase chuckled. "You guys go ahead," Chase replied.

"Let's go, dogs," Burke called. "Cooper, Pull."

I tried to jump on Cooper as we headed out into the fields, but he wouldn't have it. Sometimes Cooper forgets how to play, and this seemed to be one of those times. He pulled hard on his leash, leaning into his harness, and Burke's chair came along behind him. The wheels crunched the dry grass and fallen leaves at our feet.

I gave up on Cooper and raced ahead, picking up faint rabbit smells—this might be the day I finally caught one of the sneaky creatures! Rabbits are better to chase than squirrels, because squirrels climb trees and rabbits don't. Of course, it would be even more fun to chase either rabbits or squirrels if they understood that it was their job to be caught at the end of the chase. But they never seem to figure that part out.

It was so much fun to run and run through the fields. I loved Wenling and I loved Cooper and I loved everything else life had to offer.

"So," Burke finally said cautiously to Wenling, "I noticed you and my brother are kind of not talking to each other right now."

Wenling shrugged. "We're not mad or anything, but he's got his sports, and I need to study, and I mean, it's too early in life to get serious about a boy, really."

Burke shrugged. "Sure."

"Why, did he say something?"

"Grant? Grant never says *anything*. I'm worried he's storing up all his words and one day there will be this big explosion and everything he's never said will come blowing out and cover us in slime."

Wenling laughed. I wagged because her laughter was one of the most wonderful sounds in the world. Then

Wenling's smile left her face. "The orchard is my favorite place."

"I know, you've told me that."

"When I was a little girl, remember how you and your brother and I would play up there? And we'd eat apples and pears."

"The farm was doing pretty well then. Now, I guess this is a bad year. And last year wasn't so great, either."

"But to just chop down the trees? Really?" Wenling asked him. "Once they're gone, they're gone. So if the price of fruit goes back up, we won't have any to sell!"

"I'm sure we'd replant," Burke answered. He didn't seem too happy, either, but he wasn't as upset as Wenling.

Cooper was busy, Wenling was miserable, and Burke was solemn. Why didn't they chase rabbits with me? Why was I the only one who knew how to have fun?

"Doesn't it take four to eight years before the trees start dropping fruit? It's crazy to sell them for *wood chips*. If this is a bad year, okay, but you don't just *give up*."

Burke shrugged. "Dad says that's what farming's like. One year you rob Peter, one year you pay Paul."

"I don't know who either of those guys are! It makes no sense. You've got to tell him please don't do that. Don't cut down the trees."

Burke looked uncomfortable. "I guess the asparagus was disappointing, and the zucchini sold for less than usual . . ."

19

"Which is why you don't cut down the orchard!" Wenling interrupted. "If you do that, and you have another bad year of summer crops, you've got nothing else!"

Burke gazed at her steadily. "What's going on? It can't be just because you love the orchard so much."

Wenling took in a deep breath, then let it out slowly. "My dad says that if the farm fails, we'll have to move away."

Burke was startled. "Really? I didn't know that. Cooper, Halt."

Cooper stopped moving. He sat but still stared hard at Burke. He wasn't ready to play with me yet. I didn't know why. I had found a stick, a really nice crunchy one, and was shaking it hard. What could be better than a stick?

Well, maybe a rabbit.

"Burke, you're my best friend," Wenling said. "I don't want to move. I want to stay here."

"You're my best friend, too, Wenling."

"If they cut down the orchard, what's next? My dad getting a job in Grand Rapids?"

"Hey, that's a pretty big leap," Burke told my girl. "Just because this is a bad year doesn't mean every year will be bad. I mean, does it?"

"I don't know. I just know we have to do something," Wenling told him. "We have to save the orchard."

Burke frowned. "You do realize we're kids, right?"

"We're *smart* kids, Burke. We can think of something."

"Like what?"

"Well, I don't know what, obviously. If I knew, we wouldn't have to think of it, would we?"

"So even though your dad and my dad are working as hard as they can, you think there's something we can do to save the orchard from being cut down. Us."

"Maybe, a pair of fresh eyes might see the problem a different way," Wenling insisted.

"Different as in wrong?"

"Burke. Please. We have to try. Okay? Will you at least agree to that?"

Burke was silent for a moment. "Of course. I don't know what a couple of sixth graders can do. But yes, if you come up with something, I'll help."

After a while, we returned to where ZZ and Grant and Chase were sitting on the ground drinking from glass bottles. "Time to go, Burke," Chase said, standing up and dusting his pants.

"Thanks for your help," ZZ said to Chase.

Chase laughed. "All the things you do for me, and you're thanking me for helping you put up a gate and patching some fencing. You're something else, ZZ." Chase reached out and slapped him on the back. "You do the work of four men."

"Or women," Wenling put in.

Chase looked at Wenling and grinned. "Or women," he agreed.

"Grant is good, though," ZZ observed. I noticed Grant standing a little taller.

"Don't compliment him. He's already got a big head," Burke told ZZ.

I watched as the boys and Cooper loaded their tools into the truck.

"Bye, Wenling," Grant said. He was looking at a hammer.

"Bye, Grant," Wenling replied. She was looking at me.

Burke waved as the truck backed down the driveway, and I whined a little. As much as I loved Wenling, I was always sad to see Cooper leave.

"You need to train your dog better," ZZ told Wenling firmly. "You see how Cooper behaves? That's a well-trained animal. Lacey wants to do nothing but play."

Wenling smiled, but there was some sadness on her face, and when she spoke, I could hear it. I leaned against her leg in support. "Lacey isn't a working dog like Cooper. I know she's part boxer and that boxers can be working dogs. I read how they were bred to control cattle. But she's not all boxer. And whatever else is in there is all play, all the time. Lacey just loves to have fun."

ZZ shrugged and went inside the house. Wenling

sighed as she watched him go, and she rubbed my ears in the way that I liked so much.

"At least someone around here knows how to have fun," she whispered to me, and we went into the back-yard together.

I sniffed curiously at the tang of new wood in several sections of the fence. It was a completely different smell. All the old animal odors and the wonderful scent of mold that had been in the old fence had gone away.

I noticed when I glanced up that the new gate was yawning wide open. Wenling was busy examining something at her feet.

Through that gate, I knew, a world beckoned a dog like me, a dog who knew how to find rabbits and other wonderful things. And I felt pretty sure if I let my nose lead me, I could find my way to Cooper.

I lowered my head and trotted in the direction of that open gate. "Lacey," Wenling called from behind me. "Lacey, come here."

I paused, hesitating.

3

 "Lacey!" Wenling called more sternly. "Come *here!*"

I recognized from her tone that Wenling was getting angry. I didn't know why she was angry, but I didn't want to stick around to find out, not with freedom beckoning from the other side of that open gate. I took off running.

"Lacey," I heard Wenling wail behind me. "Lacey!"

I loved Wenling, but sometimes a dog just has to have fun.

The best part about being off leash and free is that I can track back and forth, following whatever scent beckons, learning about new places and exploring what it's like to be out in the world. I knew that my girl was running behind me, but I didn't wait for her to catch up. I was too busy smelling. Anyway, it's fun to be chased.

I didn't find Cooper right away, but I figured that eventually his scent would come to me, and I might turn in his direction if nothing more interesting lured me in another direction.

Before long, my journey led me to a noisy road. Cars were driving very fast back and forth.

I felt pretty sure that on the other side of the road, there was a river—it called to me with wonderful smells and the promise of a swim in cool water. To get there, though, I would have to make my way through these cars. They were very loud, and I wasn't sure that they would be happy to let me pass, but I felt that I had no choice. The river was just too enticing.

I steeled myself for a fast gallop, and when I judged the moment was right, I dashed across the road. As I did so, I heard a very, very loud noise. The noise moved over me like the water when I jumped off the dock into the pond. There was the same shock of complete change, of going from air to water, followed by a sense of heaviness, of pressure. When I dove beneath the surface of the pond, I always felt deaf and blind for a moment, always held my breath, and that's what happened now. Except in the pond, I was immediately back up in the sunlight, but this time it felt as if I stayed under

for a long, long time. Everything was dark, and I fell peacefully asleep.

hen I opened my eyes, I felt very much as if I were awakening from a long nap. I couldn't focus my gaze, and the jumble of smells coming through my nose told me only that I was at the vet's office, a place I had been many times before. I liked the people there. They were nice and gave me small treats. I also appreciated all the animal smells, though sometimes I could tell some of the animals were afraid. I don't know why anyone would be afraid when willing hands were giving out treats.

I struggled but found I couldn't move. I looked blearily around, trying without success to focus. I heard the woman I recognized as the vet speaking, and I could smell ZZ and Mom. I took a deeper inhalation and smelled Wenling as well. I tried to wag to let her know I knew she was in the room even if I couldn't see her, but I couldn't manage to move my tail.

This was the strangest nap I'd ever taken!

"All right." There was a weariness in her voice as the veterinarian spoke. "We've stabilized her. Lacey's not in any pain, but I have to tell you the way her vertebrae were crushed, she won't ever be able to walk on her back legs again."

I could hear and feel Wenling crying. She was in shock and pain, and I needed to get to her, yet I still couldn't move, still couldn't see. I managed to lick my lips with a dry tongue, and that was about the most I could accomplish.

After a long silence, where the only sound was Wenling's quiet sobbing, ZZ spoke gravely. "I guess, then, we should put her out of her misery. It's the right thing to do."

Wenling gasped. "*No!* No, Father, we can't do that."

Finally I was rewarded with the touch of my girl's hand on my head. I blinked, trying to see her. Her face appeared to me as if she were standing on the dock and I was beneath the surface of the pond—I could barely make her out. As she petted my fur, I could feel her fingers trembling. She was upset, and I still couldn't fully wake up to help her. I pictured chasing a ball, rolling on my back, barking with joy— all things I could do to make her feel better. I just needed to *move!*

I heard Mom murmur, "ZZ, please." Then she spoke more loudly. "I don't think we have to make that decision yet, do we, Doctor? We can wait."

"Oh no," the vet replied. "I don't think you need to rush a decision like this. There's no sigh of internal bleeding, and I've sewed shut her wounds. She let me probe the entire area—there's no pain. It's just that when she recovers, she won't be able to use her legs."

"LiMin, a dog who can't walk is of no use," ZZ argued. "We can't—"

"I think," Mom interrupted firmly, "we should see how things go the next couple of days. Don't you, ZZ?" Mom turned to Wenling. "Honey, why don't you go wait in the car? We'll be out shortly, and we'll bring Lacey with us, I promise."

Sniffling, Wenling left the room—I didn't see it, but I felt it. I did not like that she was sad, and I did not like that she was leaving me, but there didn't seem to be anything I could do about it. I couldn't even wake up.

"The dog has a broken back," ZZ insisted.

"Yes, I know," Mom said. "But can you see how this is affecting your daughter? Let's just let Lacey come home, and we'll see how it goes. If she's suffering, Wenling will understand what we need to do. But you can't ask her to make that decision now. Our daughter's been through enough already for one day."

There was another long silence. "You are right," ZZ finally replied.

I was very happy when I was carried to the car in ZZ's strong arms. He set me on the back seat, and Wenling cradled my head in her lap. I wanted to kiss her and let her know that I was still her happy dog, but I was still finding it very difficult to move. I fell asleep as soon as the car began moving.

For the next several days, I was tied with several leashes to my bed. The only time I was ever allowed out was when Wenling untied me, carried me to the backyard, and set me down to do my business. When she left in the morning she would whisper, "I'll come right home after school, I promise," and I would lie in my bed and sleep.

My legs were being very silly. My front paws still touched the ground and moved normally, but my back legs were flopping all over the place. In fact, I had to keep checking to make sure that they were even there. Wenling stood behind me and held me in a squatting position, something I could see but not feel.

"Oh, Lacey," Wenling said mournfully. "I'm so sorry."

Mom came out to watch us. "Why don't you let me carry Lacey or wait for your dad to come home?" she suggested. "She's a little heavy for you."

Wenling shook her head. "No, I have to show Dad that I know how to take care of Lacey myself. Otherwise, he'll want to put Lacey to sleep."

Mom frowned. "I don't think that's true, honey."

"No," Wenling insisted. "I know Dad. It's true."

Making matters worse, Wenling had decided to

dress me up. This often happened in the winter when she would stuff my front paws into a scratchy, soft material and then laugh at me and tell me I was dressed like Santa. She would even put something floppy on my head. I put up with this because I loved Wenling.

Now, though, my outfit was made up of a stiff, hard cone around my neck. I was very itchy along my back and needed her to remove this cone so I could lick the area properly, but she would not.

Days and days passed like this. I loved Wenling and would tolerate just about anything if she was nearby, but I was going out of my mind, strapped to the bed, lying there all the time. I needed to get up and run and play! That's what a dog does.

I was so happy when she finally unbound me from the elaborate system of leashes. At last I could run!

Except I couldn't. Again, my front paws seemed to know exactly what to do, but my rear end—that was different. All I could do was drag myself along the floor on my stomach. It was as if I no longer had back legs! But when I turned to check, they were there, along with my short tail.

The shiny, slick floors in the living room made for easy going once I learned to just pull myself along. I had more difficulty on the carpet, though. Just a few runs across the rug and my stomach was sore. I decided to stay away from the carpet for the time being.

Until my legs stopped being so silly, I would put up with whatever I needed to in order to be with my Wenling, who still carried me outside several times a day, grunting in my ear. She would hold my back end up while I did my business. People do strange things, and all dogs can do is go along with whatever it is.

I was overjoyed one sunny afternoon when Chase drove his truck up the driveway and I smelled Cooper inside. The door opened and Chase set Burke's chair on the ground, and Burke slid into it. Cooper bounded out and I yipped joyously, but then I recognized Cooper was in one of his moods.

I did not understand why these moods happened, but I was used to it by now. Completely serious, completely focused on Burke, Cooper would act as if he'd forgotten that a dog's real job is to play. Nothing I could do would entice him into a game of Chase or Tug on a Stick.

Burke fastened one end of Cooper's leash to his chair. I watched as Cooper solemnly pulled Burke across the dead grasses of the front yard. I wondered if Cooper could tell from the smell in the air that the days were getting steadily colder and that soon he and I would be able to frolic in the snow that would lie heavy on the ground. This was what we always did in the winter. One of my favorite things about Cooper was how much he loved the snow.

When they reached the steps, Burke slid out of his

chair, grabbed Cooper's harness, and said the word *Assist*. Wenling never said this word to me, so I never bothered to react to it. But to Cooper, it meant to slowly make his way toward us, step by step, with Burke pushing himself along, holding on to Cooper's harness.

At the top step, I wanted to leap on Cooper and play with him, but even if my back legs would let me, I could tell that he was not having any of it. His stare was cold.

ZZ had come out to watch all this, and now he said to Burke, "That is a well-trained animal." For some reason, when he said this, everyone but Cooper looked at me. I looked back, wondering if they were about to give me some treats. Or maybe a squeaky toy?

Burke slipped into his chair when ZZ brought it up the steps from the yard. He slapped his hands together. "Okay, Cooper!" he announced.

And with that, Cooper was back to being a normal dog, immediately frisky and pawing at me. I loved Cooper, but he could be very silly sometimes. Thankfully he always stopped being silly when Burke said, "Okay!"

It was so frustrating not to be able to climb on Cooper and race around the yard, tearing up dead grass with our paws. I whined and squirmed over onto my back. Cooper nosed at me and nibbled my face gently.

"Your mom needs you," ZZ told Wenling.

"Oh." Wenling sprang to her feet. "Would you watch the dog?" she asked Burke.

"Of course."

Cooper and I both heard the word *dog* but by now, I was busy chewing on *his* face, and I didn't want to stop what I was doing. ZZ stood quietly for a moment as Wenling went into the house. "You did a good job training your dog," he finally commented.

"I had to work with him a lot," Burke replied. "He didn't really understand at first that I needed him to do an important job for me, but dogs like to work. They like to have a purpose. Once he figured it out, he became the best dog ever."

ZZ was silent for a moment. Then he took a deep breath. "I would like your help, Burke."

Burke cocked his head. "Yeah?"

"I am trying to explain to Wenling that it isn't right, what's happening with Lacey. We can't pretend all is normal. She will never recover. She will never be able to walk again. She is a dog who must now drag herself across the floor. What kind of life is that?"

"Well . . . ," Burke started to reply, but ZZ wasn't finished.

"We should put Lacey down," ZZ concluded. "It's the decent thing to do."

4

Cooper and I both froze because Burke had just inhaled sharply. Cooper broke off play to go to him. I wasn't done wrestling, and I dragged myself over to my friend. He ignored me, eyes on his boy.

"See?" ZZ said softly. "What kind of life can Lacey ever have now?"

Burke thought about it. Cooper remained focused on him, ignoring me completely. It was as if he'd forgotten that he'd heard Burke say, "Okay!" I pawed at him to remind him that it was playtime.

"I'm not sure what you're asking me, ZZ."

"Wenling can be stubborn. I don't know how to talk to her without her getting upset with me. But you're her friend. She will listen to you."

"So you want to put her dog to sleep? I'm not sure she'll listen to that from anybody."

"Lacey can't be happy like this," ZZ insisted.

Burke turned his chair slightly. "Do you think I'm not happy, ZZ?"

ZZ stiffened. "I did not mean that. You are not a dog. You understand."

"Well, you're right. Dogs aren't like people," Burke agreed. "Cooper just kind of . . . lives in the moment. Lacey probably does, too."

Cooper and I both looked up at Burke, wondering why he had just said our names.

"I'm sure Lacey doesn't remember being hit by a car," Burke continued, "and now she just accepts that she can't move her legs. It's like how dogs accept living in a new home or having to eat different food or something. She's probably already moved on. A person who can't walk, they might . . ." He paused for just a second. "They might spend years being sad about that. Or mad. Or whatever. But dogs, they don't do that."

ZZ was silent.

"Look, Lacey's not in pain, sir. Give her a chance. Doesn't everybody deserve that? I mean, I'm in a wheelchair. And when I was younger, I didn't like being different from the other kids, but then I got Cooper. And now I get to have my best friend in the world with me, helping me get through school each day. And other things, too. I couldn't be happier. Shouldn't we give Lacey a chance to be happy, too?"

Burke and ZZ stood quietly for a moment. People are like dogs in that way—they don't always have to be making noise. They can sit quietly, just like dogs do.

Though if a squirrel runs past, dogs know what to do, but people don't even *react*.

Wenling returned and I felt as if I were wagging, but when I checked, my tail was limp behind my splayed legs.

"Thank you, Burke," ZZ said. He passed Wenling and went into the house.

"What did he thank you for?" Wenling asked curiously.

Burke shrugged. "He says you're a wild child but that I calm you down and keep you from being arrested."

"Very funny."

"So did you figure out how we can save the orchard yet? You've had a couple of weeks. By now I thought you'd probably made a plan to build flying cars."

Wenling sighed. "No, not really. We're not legally allowed to have jobs yet, except we could referee kids' sports. Which I don't know how to do. Or caddy at the golf club—we can do that."

"*You* can do that, maybe," Burke replied doubtfully. "And it's probably not the best time of year to start a caddy business. It's already fall. I don't know how much longer the golf course will still be open. And to be a caddy, don't you have to understand something about, I don't know, *golf*?"

Wenling shook her head in frustration. "I think golf is really boring."

"You know you'll be popular with the golfers when they find out you don't know anything about the sport except you think it's boring," Burke said. "Why hire a professional caddy when you could have someone like that?"

"We are allowed to start our own business, though," Wenling told him.

"That's great!" Burke seemed excited, but he wasn't really. Dogs can tell. "I've always wanted to run an aerospace company. Or maybe I could do international finance."

"One time I had that lemonade stand, remember?"

"Yeah. It was the worst lemonade *ever*. It was like sour water with ice."

"Plus the only reason I made money is that I didn't have to pay for any of the ingredients."

"The only reason you made money is your parents bought some and then poured it out when you weren't looking."

"It's hopeless," Wenling muttered in disgust. "Why do I think I can do anything? You were right the first time. I'm just a kid."

Burke shook his head. "No! That's not like you, Wenling. Don't give up. You'll think of something. You said it:

you're really smart. We just need the right idea. Something that's not an aerospace company and not a lemonade stand."

Burke and Wenling became silent. I looked at Cooper, and Cooper looked at me. Then Burke brightened. "I know!" he exclaimed. "We could open a dog training business."

Cooper was still ignoring me, and I'd had enough. I climbed up on his back. It was tough, dragging my legs behind me, but I got up far enough to gnaw on his neck.

Wenling watched me sadly. "I'm not sure—" she started to say. Then she took a deep gulping breath. "I'm not sure I'd be any good at that," she finished in a rush.

My girl was upset! I fell off Cooper and squirmed over to thrust my nose underneath her hand. I knew she'd feel better if she petted me. She always did.

Wenling didn't just pet me; she sat down on the floor, pulled me into her lap, and hugged me, burying her face in the fur around my neck. "The whole reason Lacey got hurt was because I couldn't even train her to come when I call!" she said miserably.

"Hey," Burke said gently. "Hey, Wenling, don't say that. It was an accident. Accidents happen."

We were all quiet together. I panted a little because it's hard work getting around when your legs aren't cooperating, and because it was warm, being hugged by my girl.

"Anyway," Burke said. "Dog training is a lot of work. Took me more than a year to train Cooper. So we'll come up with something else."

Wenling took her face out of my neck. "We have to."

"I know."

"Don't tell anybody what we're doing, okay? I don't want my dad or your dad finding out we're trying to think of a way to save the orchard."

Burke gave her a crooked grin. "I know you probably don't believe this, but my dad isn't looking to us to do anything but just go to school and be, I don't know, kids. It's really not our responsibility to try to save anything, Wenling."

Wenling stared at Burke, then shook her head. "So one minute you tell me not to give up, and then the next you tell me not to try. Which is it?"

"I mean, I'm just trying to say the right thing here."

Wenling turned and walked into the house, and I flinched when she slammed the door behind her. I anxiously eyed Burke, the lone human left on the porch. My person had just abandoned me, and he was the only one who could fix it!

I dragged myself over to the front door and put my nose to the bottom crack and inhaled. I could smell my girl in there. What was she doing? Her dog was out here!

I felt the vibration as footsteps approached the door

from the other side. I could tell it wasn't Wenling, though. The footfalls were too heavy. Just before the door opened, the scent told me it was ZZ.

He carefully eased his way out, making sure he didn't step on me. He reached out and touched Burke's chair. "I noticed at your father's farm, in the barn, there is a chair just like this one, only smaller," he said.

Burke nodded. "I had that one when I was pretty young."

"Does the chair belong to you?" ZZ asked. "Or does it belong to your father?"

"No," Burke explained, "it's mine. I got it for Christmas. I can still remember unwrapping the package. I had another chair on loan from a hospital supply company, but it was old and heavy. The new one was lighter, way easier to push. Why? Why do you want to know?"

A few days later, I was playing with Wenling in the living room, though the game wasn't very fun. She was holding out her hand and saying, "Stay."

I had heard that word before but never really understood what it meant or how it applied to me—especially since Wenling kept saying it in such a stern fashion. It seemed like she couldn't really be talking to me. Who could be cross with me? I was the fun dog!

Because her hand was outstretched, I thought for a moment she meant for me to remain lying on the floor in front of her. But when she started to back away, I knew that couldn't be the case. Wenling would always want to be with me.

"Stay," she commanded. I figured this was the same as Come, so I happily pulled myself across the floor toward her.

"Oh, Lacey," Wenling said mournfully. There was unhappiness in her voice. I knew that, even though it had just been for a moment, being a few steps apart from me had somehow made her sad. I reached her and licked her legs to cheer her up. Yes, we had been apart, but now we were back together!

Mom came into the room. "How's the dog training going?"

Wenling shook her head. "Lacey doesn't understand anything I'm trying to teach her."

"Want a break? Your dad would like you and Lacey to meet him in the garage."

"Really? Sure! Come on, Lacey." Wenling stood and gathered me into her arms. She had been carrying me around a lot lately and no longer huffed and grunted with the effort. I didn't know why she insisted on carrying me these days—she never used to do it. But I loved the feeling of my girl's arms around me. Sometimes she would bury her face in my fur as we walked.

The day was brisk and cool as we stepped outside and crossed the yard to the smaller house where the car usually sat. ZZ liked to spend time in there playing with metal toys and wood.

Wenling carried me over the threshold and set me down on the cold cement floor. Pulling myself along here was not as easy as in the living room, but it was better than when I tried to cross rough rugs.

ZZ wordlessly pointed to something that looked similar to the kind of chair Burke sat in, the one Cooper sometimes liked to pull. Except there was no chair part, just wheels and what appeared to be a harness between them. I sniffed suspiciously.

"What is it?" Wenling asked.

"I bought Burke's first wheelchair from him and used the wheels to make Lacey this cart," ZZ explained. "See? I put in tethers to hold her in place. She can now walk with her front paws on the ground and her back supported by this wheeled cart."

Wenling clapped her hands together, and I glanced up at her in surprise. Her mouth was open, as were her eyes, and then she grinned. She ran across the floor and threw herself at her father, who enveloped her in his arms. ZZ was smiling, and I reflected that I did not see him smile very much. ZZ was as serious as Cooper in one of his moods.

"Lacey! You've got your own wheelchair!" Wenling told me.

I didn't know what she was saying, but it obviously made her happier than Stay. Stay never makes anybody happy.

"This," she declared, "is going to change everything!"

5

Cooper came over with Burke a short time later. ZZ had pulled the wheeled thing, which Wenling kept calling a *cart,* out into the yard and had hoisted my back legs into it. I was not sure what to make of this new development. I couldn't see precisely what was going on without twisting myself, and whenever I did that, Wenling reached out and put her hands on the cart.

"No, Lacey," she told me. "Don't tip over the cart."

In this instance, I felt pretty sure that *no* meant "you're doing something wrong," so it was particularly frustrating that she wouldn't let me turn around so I could figure out what it was.

ZZ was back in the house when Burke and Cooper came up the driveway in Chase's car. Cooper and

I stared at each other through the window, astounded that he was taking a car ride and I wasn't.

After all three of them got out of the car, Chase went into the house while Burke and Cooper came over to greet me.

"Wow," Burke said, "that looks great! Your dad is really good at stuff like this."

Wenling nodded. "We haven't tried moving yet. I'm just trying to get her to hold still in the cart. Not going well."

"Okay, I'll hold on to her while you go over there. Call her, and we'll see how she does," Burke suggested.

I watched in concern as Wenling walked away from me. She strolled to the end of the driveway and turned to face us. Burke held his hand on my collar, which I figured meant I wasn't supposed to go anywhere, even though he wasn't my actual person. Cooper was doing Sit next to his boy and, even with no hand on his collar, was motionless, his focus on Burke. Cooper was in one of his moods.

When Burke's hand released my collar, I knew I needed to run to Wenling even though she wasn't calling me. Dogs belong with their people.

I dashed to Wenling, moving shockingly fast. I didn't understand it, but my stomach was no longer touching the ground. And I could *run*!

Joyfully, I twisted and turned, my front paws coming

off the ground, so happy that I didn't need to drag my stomach down the driveway. Then I heard a noise, and my whole body was flipped onto its side as if ZZ had reached out with his strong arms and wrenched me over. Dazed and bewildered, I tried to scramble to my feet. Now my body felt pinned, and the cart was lying sideways.

"Stop! *Stop!*" Wenling shouted. I didn't know what she meant, but, upon hearing the distress in her voice, I did my best to claw my way to her. The cart held me back, making a grinding noise on the surface of the driveway as I struggled. Wenling reached me and grabbed my collar.

Burke wheeled himself over next to me. "Okay, that didn't go particularly well," he observed dryly.

Wenling shook her head. "Lacey's always been such a high-energy dog."

"Look," Burke continued, "there's a first time for everything. Remember when we played wheelchair basketball in the barn? Pretty much nobody but me could move, especially when we just got started. It's Lacey's first time in the cart, so of course she's going to have issues. Let's give it another shot."

Wenling picked me up, and as she did so, the cart came with me, tied to my torso with leashes. Then I was conscious of both wheels touching down on the driveway. She pulled some straps that tugged on me a little. I tried to twist to figure out what she was doing, but Burke snagged my collar.

Cooper watched all of this without changing expression. Sometimes I think he pretends to understand things that he actually doesn't.

"Okay, I think she's ready. Let's try it again," Wenling suggested.

There was a certain tense unhappiness being shared by Burke and Wenling, and I knew the way to cheer them up. A good tearing around the yard, perhaps accompanied by barking, would make them laugh and clap their hands. Burke might tell Cooper, "Okay," and my best friend would join me, enjoying being a dog.

As soon as Burke released me, I pivoted and dashed for the grass. Immediately, I was stopped short and, once again, my whole body was twisted and thrown to the ground.

What kind of game were we playing?

"Oh no," Wenling moaned. I tried to get up, thinking the sadness was getting worse. I really, really needed to race around and bring joy to the situation. But then Wenling was there, her arms steadying me and, once again, the wheels were placed on the ground. "She's not getting it," Wenling declared mournfully.

"Well, wait, I have an idea," Burke offered as he wheeled himself up. Burke called Cooper who came instantly. Cooper sniffed at me, and I licked him in the face, but he was doing his whole focused thing, his eyes back on Burke.

Cooper would have a lot more fun if he just learned to relax.

"So you know Cooper can do Pull when I need him to help me through snow or whatever," Burke told Wenling, who nodded. "So let's try doing the same thing with Lacey."

Sometimes when people say dogs' names over and over, the treats will come out, but even though I could smell some beef bits in Burke's pocket, he didn't reach for anything.

Burke took the two leashes that were coiled on Cooper's harness and stretched them out past me. He clipped them to the straps on the cart behind me. "There. Now, what will happen is Cooper will pull Lacey, and Lacey will understand how she needs to move to keep the cart from falling over."

"Good idea," Wenling agreed enthusiastically. "Cooper, you're going to teach Lacey how to walk!"

"Cooper," Burke called softly, "come here. *Come.*" Cooper maneuvered himself until he was standing directly in front of me, his tail nearly touching my face. I had sniffed that area of his body many times before and wasn't interested in doing it again at that moment. "All right, Cooper, Pull," Burke commanded.

I'd heard that word a lot in my life, but it never applied to me. *Pull* was a word for Cooper only.

Now, though, as Cooper surged steadily forward, I

felt as if I were being dragged. I was forced to move my front feet to keep from falling onto my face. We took a few steps this way, and then I decided I was tired of the view. I twisted away, jumping sideways, and crashed to the ground. Cooper halted immediately, and I looked up at him, utterly confused.

Had he done that? Why did it seem every step I took wound up with me lying on my side? Was this what Wenling meant by *Cart*?

I decided I did not like the game of Cart. I'd rather play with Cooper and then enjoy some beef bits.

It was not meant to be. Instead, we spent most of the day with Cooper being his not-a-dog self, focused only on doing the same thing over and over again, which was to stand in front of me while I tried to dart around him and got flung to the dirt by the cart.

I knew that I loved Cooper and would always love Cooper, but I was really getting sick of his attitude. If he would just stop sticking his butt in my face, maybe I'd stop falling over.

"I think," Burke finally suggested, "that Cooper is doing his work, and he *loves* to do work. Dogs want to have a job, but Lacey's never done work before and doesn't know what it is. Up until now, she's only played."

"I'll make sure she works," Wenling vowed. "We'll do this every single day until she gets it."

Burke regarded her carefully. "Would it be the end of the world if she doesn't figure it out?"

"My dad made this cart for her."

"I know, but . . . life's full of disappointments, right? I mean, I wanted a fun brother, but I wound up with Grant."

Wenling gazed levelly at Burke. "If this doesn't work, Lacey will never be able to go for a walk with me again. She'll have to be carried out to the yard whenever she needs to do her business. She'll only be able to go into places with smooth floors, because when she drags herself on carpet, it hurts her stomach. What kind of life is that for a dog?"

"Are you saying what I think you're saying? Because it would be a life. She would still be loved by you, and she would love you back. Isn't that the most important thing a dog does? Cooper's a working dog, and he helps me do so many things. But even if he didn't do that, I'd still love him. And he'd love me. And that would be his most important job."

"I know." Wenling rubbed her eyes. "But she was such a happy, fun-loving dog. Seeing her with her back legs out behind her breaks my heart. My dad says this is one of the most important things we do for our dogs: we put them to sleep when they're suffering. Her stomach can't take getting scraped up all the time. And you can see how much she wants to run, and she can't. She just can't."

Burke considered this, then nodded. "It will be the hardest decision you ever have to make in your life."

Wenling sighed. "I know. That's why I want to keep training and training until she gets it." She let out a long, wobbling sigh. "It's my fault that Lacey escaped the yard."

"Wenling, come on," Burke said softly. "Don't keep saying that."

"But I have to make it up to her, Burke! Training her to use the cart, that's the only way I can do that."

Burke nodded. "Okay. I don't think having Cooper pull is helping the way I thought it would, though."

My ears perked up, because Burke had said *Okay*. And *Okay* was his word meaning "Cooper can go back to being a normal dog." But Cooper didn't even blink. He just kept his eyes on Burke. Like all words, the use of *Okay* could change with how it was said.

Later, Wenling unstrapped me from the cart and lifted me to the ground, and Burke said, "Okay," the right way, and Cooper and I wrestled in the grass.

That was the last time I had any fun for a long, long time. The next day and the next and the next were dismally the same. Wenling carried me out to the driveway and put me in the cart. She strapped me down. She told me to do Stay, which I still didn't understand, and then she would take a few steps away. But when she looked back, I knew she needed me and I would dash to her, and the cart would drag and pull me down with it.

We would repeat this until my front paws were trembling with the effort and Wenling's sadness bore down on her, making her shoulders slump. Obviously, something was going wrong, but it wasn't something I could understand.

At night, I had dreams about that cart. In them, I was always falling, always being pulled around by the thing and flung on my side.

Another day, and another, spent doing the same thing. It was what Wenling wanted, so I gamely went along, because she was my person and I loved her. It wasn't making her happy, but it was all she cared about.

Mom came out to watch. I proudly showed her how I had learned that I could dart and turn and pull that cart over with almost no effort. It was just what we were doing now. "The cart's getting a little beaten up," Mom observed.

Wenling nodded. "Yeah, Dad already had to adjust the wheels a couple of times. I don't understand. Lacey just keeps doing the same thing. I've tried scolding her. I've tried giving her treats. I've tried giving her love. She just doesn't get it. She almost seems to *like* pulling the cart over."

Mom pursed her lips. "I've been watching you from the front window. You don't give up, Wenling."

Wenling shrugged.

"No, I mean it," Mom continued. "I really admire how

hardworking you are. You're just like your father. You'll keep at something until you figure it out. It's a trait not too many other people have. Most people would have given up by now, but not you."

"Okay," Wenling replied.

Mom smiled. "That is so like your father, to say *okay*. You know, I've known your father a long time, and he goes to work every day, and I know he works hard and sometimes he comes home so exhausted he can barely have his dinner, and he does that day after day. When the crops need to be harvested, when the zucchini is growing too fast in the fields, he'll work until long after sunset and then get up the next morning and do that for twenty days in a row. But it affects him. He gets tired. He becomes moody, and his other jobs, things that he always tends to around the house, are neglected. When I see that happening, do you know what I do?"

Wenling shook her head.

"I tell him it's time to go fishing."

Wenling laughed. "*What?*"

Mom nodded. "I tell him I want to go fishing. He'll say he's got too much work to do, but I put my foot down. He knows better than to argue with me when I decide it's time to fish. We'll pack up the rods, drop you at Chase's house to spend a night or two, and go to the river. And we'll stand there and fish, or we'll get on a boat and go out on the lake."

"Well, sure," Wenling said, puzzled. "I mean, I know you love fishing."

Mom grinned and shook her head. "Oh no, I *hate* fishing."

Wenling stared at her mother.

6

"I don't understand what you're saying, Mom. You always want to go fishing. You're telling me you don't like it?" Wenling demanded.

"No, honey, I'm saying I *hate* it. You just sit there looking at a thin line in the water, waiting for a tug on your rod. Times like those, I'd kill to get my hands on a book."

"Then why do you do it?"

"Because," Mom explained, "it relaxes your father. I watch the tension ease out of him. He'll take a nap in the middle of the day, and when he goes back to the farm, he's got his old energy back. He smiles. Haven't you noticed how, when we get back from a fishing trip, he's in such a good mood?"

I yawned. This was better than playing Tip the Cart,

but I thought if the humans were just going to stand around and talk, Wenling should unstrap me and put me in the grass so I could sleep.

"So maybe," Mom concluded, "you should try something like that with Lacey."

"Take her fishing?" Wenling asked with a smile.

"Well, not that. But you said she seemed stuck doing the same behavior over and over, and it reminded me that's how I sometimes think of ZZ. He gets stuck. I wonder if maybe Lacey would work harder if you took breaks, because, right now, she seems miserable and you seem miserable, and I don't see how that's helping."

Wenling regarded me thoughtfully. I sighed. Mom turned away. "Mom?" Wenling said in a small voice.

Mom turned back with a questioning look.

"Dad's tired *now*."

"He's exhausted from working the farm, falling asleep right after dinner, then waking up to go to that restaurant and close the kitchen for the night. It's a lot of work."

"He isn't doing that for *me*, is he?" Wenling asked. I snapped my eyes to hers because of the anguish I heard in her voice. "I know I said I didn't want to move, but not if it means Dad works himself to death."

Mom gave Wenling a kind smile. "No, honey. Not for you, not for me, not even for this house. Your father has thrown everything he has into that farm, and he wants to give it as long as he can before they call it quits. He's stubborn, just like you."

"I know they want to sell the orchard trees for wood chips," Wenling replied in a rush, "but don't you think that's a bad idea? Some years, the orchard makes more money than anything else."

Mom regarded Wenling thoughtfully. "I think," she finally responded slowly, "that your father would only cut down those trees as a last resort. Same with Chase. If they do wind up taking down those trees, it means we've come to the very end of our rope."

I was so excited the next day when Wenling and I rode with ZZ in his truck. My nose told me we were going to Cooper's farm and, sure enough, there we were.

Burke said, "Okay," and Cooper ran to us wagging and play bowing and being a normal dog. Wenling carried me down to the pond. The ducks squawked in alarm as we approached and finally decided they were better off on the other side of the pond. That, of course, was the proper thing for them to do.

"So what's the plan?" Burke asked.

Wenling held out her arms, and Burke wordlessly handed her what looked like a big coat. It was puffy and had straps on it. "So I'm going to put the life jacket around her middle. She'll have to paddle with her front legs, but her back legs won't sink," Wenling explained. She set me down and wrapped me in the coat. I was worried it meant I would soon be wearing a silly hat.

Cooper watched all of this curiously. When Wenling was finished, she stepped back to admire her work. "So, Lacey, you want to go swimming?"

I was wagging, though of course my silly tail was motionless. I was happy because I had a sense of what was to happen next.

Burke commanded, "Cooper, Stay," and Cooper immediately dropped out of fun dog mode. Was that what *Stay* meant? "Stop having fun"? If so, I liked *Stay* about as much as I liked *no*. Why do people even need such words, when there are so many wonderful things to say, like *good dog* and *treat*?

Wenling carried me out into the water up to her knees and then gently set me down. The water was very cold, but it felt good. I was energized. I immediately took off swimming, turning in a wide circle.

I was happy. It had been so long since I'd been in the pond!

"Cooper," Burke called. Burke cranked his arm back and threw a ball. A *ball*! There was a huge splash as Cooper hit the water. Cooper was a very strong dog and swam faster than I could, but I was already out in the pond. I began digging at the water with my front paws, paddling so hard that my shoulders rose up above the surface. I could sense Cooper approaching, but I did not glance at him.

I got to the ball first and snatched it. Cooper came up, sniffed me, and then swam in a circle around me, concerned that I had the ball and that he might never get his mouth on it. I swam straight to Wenling and opened my mouth when my front paws touched the sandy bottom of the pond.

Wenling reached down and picked up the ball. I stared at it and could sense Cooper doing the same thing. "Ready?" Wenling asked. She whipped her arm and threw the ball back out into the pond.

Instantly, Cooper and I were after it. Cooper was swimming at a slight angle because I was to his side, and he was forcing me to make a wide, slow turn, and he got to the ball first. I swam near him, hoping he'd drop it, but he didn't.

The next time, though, Burke threw a ball, and so did Wenling. Now Cooper and I each had a ball! Of course, we both wanted to get both of them.

I swam to the first one, grabbed it, and then turned to go for the second one, and my head dipped underwater. I pulled back up spluttering and dropped the ball.

I did not understand what had just happened. I had merely been twisting around to get the other ball, and then somehow I'd lost them both. Cooper had a ball

in his mouth and was swimming around, bumping the other ball with his nose.

I dug in the water and went after him, and when he turned, I turned, too, and my head went under again. I pulled up. This was completely unexpected, and I wasn't too happy about it. I'd never had this problem before!

Luckily, Cooper still couldn't get both balls in his mouth. That didn't prevent him from trying, though.

I finally made it over to him and grabbed the ball in my own mouth. When I went to return to Wenling, however, I made a wider turn, and my head did not go underwater. That was the secret to this game, and it's how I played the rest of the day. Cooper and I would both plunge out into the pond to pursue one or both balls. When I went to turn, if I tried to change direction too swiftly, my head would go under. So I learned to take wide, slower turns to make my way back to Wenling.

Finally, Cooper struggled out of the pond with a ball and, instead of taking it to Burke, went up on shore, flopped down on his belly, and chewed on it. He was done chasing balls for the time being. I was pretty tired, too, but I was having fun with Wenling. She was no longer sad. I would do this all day long if it made her happy. I was a normal dog, not a moody one like Cooper.

"It's okay, Lacey," Wenling told me. She let me keep

the ball, and I exhaustedly flopped down in the squishy coat I was wearing, which held my stomach up off the ground in a funny way. "Sometimes, to do work, a dog needs to play first," Wenling explained.

Burke smiled. "It's been a long time since I first trained Cooper, and I forgot, but you're right. If it's all work and no play, then . . ." Burke shrugged. "You stop getting results. Dogs are like people. They can burn out."

For some reason, both Burke and Wenling looked up at the farmhouse and the barn when he said this.

"How is your dad doing?" Wenling asked softly.

Burke shrugged. "He's worried about money. But he's decided to see if he can sell the harvest from the orchard before he cuts down the trees. I guess the baby food company is paying a little more than they did last year. He said that makes a difference, even if it's just pennies."

"That's good. But then what?"

Burke looked at Wenling. "He says we won't starve. The land is worth something. We'll pull up stakes and go somewhere."

"My mom says we'll know it's all over when they cut down the trees. It will mean they're giving up."

"So then, that's good news. Gives us until spring to think of something," Burke reasoned.

"It's so unfair. If we were older, we could get jobs, help pay expenses."

"You're forgetting about my aerospace company," Burke reminded her. "That's going to make billions."

Wenling didn't smile. "My mom says Dad would be fine working in a factory, but I think it would kill him. All he's ever known is farming."

"I'm sorry, Wenling. I don't know what we can do."

Wenling didn't reply right away. Then she blurted, "Snow shoveling!"

"What do you mean?"

"When it snows, I can shovel the neighbors' driveways and make money that way."

"People get their driveways plowed, Wenling."

"Well, then, I'll shovel the sidewalks where the plows can't reach."

"Yeah, except that the snowplow drivers do that as part of their jobs."

"Then I'll work for the snowplow drivers," Wenling declared insistently.

"But then you'd have a job. You said that was illegal."

Wenling stamped her foot on the ground. "You're not helping, Burke! Why don't you come up with your own ideas instead of trashing mine!"

I cringed because Wenling was angry. Cooper gave Burke a concerned look but didn't otherwise react. Both people were silent for a moment.

"I'm sorry," Burke murmured softly.

And then neither one of our people said anything else for a long while.

I expected that the next day would be spent in the driveway doing our cart-tipping game, but I was wrong. Wenling sat in front of the fireplace, and I lay with my head in her lap. She held a dry-smelling object and touched her fingertips to it frequently.

"What are you reading?" Mom asked.

Wenling held up the thing she was holding. "It's about a dog who lives a lot of different lives," she replied.

"Is it any good?"

"Like, the best book ever."

"No training for Lacey today?"

I glanced lazily at Mom because she'd said my name.

"I'm letting her go fishing today," Wenling replied with a smile.

The next day, Cooper and Burke came over again. I was seeing a lot more of them recently, and that made me very happy. We walked out into the driveway, and Wenling lifted me into the cart and strapped me down.

This again?

"Okay, Cooper!" Burke called.

Cooper instantly broke from his focus on Burke and turned to me. I was conscious of the fact that Wenling clearly wanted me to tip the cart, but I was so tired of being slammed to the ground. I held still, letting Cooper climb on me and paw me and chew my face. When he pranced away, I couldn't help myself and took a few steps forward. The cart stayed upright, rolling smoothly. As long as I didn't try to turn, I could move! This hadn't occurred to me before.

But Cooper didn't know about only walking, no running. He dashed around, having fun, and I wanted to join him! When he ran to the side, I instinctively turned toward him in a wide circle, remembering that a sharp twist had sent my head underwater when I'd been in the pond. A wide turn was better there. Maybe here, too?

"Yes, Lacey!" Wenling shouted excitedly.

Startled, I stopped and glanced at her. I was glad she was happy and was glad she was calling my name, but didn't know if I was being praised for something specific or just for being a wonderful dog.

Then it occurred to me: the point of being here was to crash the cart onto its side, not to chase Cooper. I'd learned that from many days of practice.

Though I was less than fond of that game, I knew it was what my girl wanted. I twisted sharply, deliberately cutting a tight turn, and was rewarded with a perfect cart crash.

"Oh, Lacey. Oh no," Wenling moaned.

She trudged up to me, and I looked up, hoping for a treat. Her arms came down to lift me onto my legs, but instead of releasing me for another game of Tip the Cart, she just knelt there, her arms around me, face in my fur. "I really thought you'd figure it out, Lacey."

I loved being held by my girl, but the sadness was coming out of her in a flood. I panted, distressed that I wasn't able to help her.

7

Burke wheeled up to Wenling. I glanced at him, and he seemed sad, too. I figured that what needed to happen was for Wenling to let me go so I could tip the cart over again, but she held me tightly.

"Don't give up hope, Wenling," Burke murmured.

Wenling looked up at him, her eyes full of tears. Her smile was trembling. "It's all going bad, isn't it? Lacey's never going to understand this. We're going to have to put her to sleep. And maybe they don't cut the orchard down right now, because they've managed to make it through the fall. But they'll chop down the trees in the spring, and that will mean we're moving and the farm is being sold."

Burke took in a deep breath, then let it out. "I can't explain why, but I think you're wrong. I don't think it's all bad. I think we'll come up with something, or at least you'll come up with something, that'll help us save the orchard. I really do, Wenling. And Lacey's so close, can't you see that? She knows how to turn without falling over, but she just forgets. Hey, I have an idea."

Wenling gave him a wooden gaze.

"Come on," Burke insisted. "Here's what you do. Start walking with Lacey, holding her collar, in big circles. Give her treats. Then let go of her collar but keep going in circles, okay? Run a little faster. Keep giving her treats, keep turning, until she turns on her own!"

"We tried something like that already," Wenling objected.

"But we both saw what happened in the pond. Lacey learned how to turn without getting dunked, because she wanted the ball. Same thing with treats."

I was very encouraged to hear my name and the word *treats* repeated several times. When Wenling began strolling around in the yard, I went willingly, and I didn't even mind her hand on my collar because of the small treats she fed me. Cooper came over, feeling that if treats were being handed out, he obviously deserved one, but instantly responded and ran to Burke when he said, "Come."

This was a new game, full of opportunities to eat treats. I could easily keep up with Wenling, even when she started jogging. I was right next to her, nose up and ready for any treats she might be offering.

Soon we were turning wide loops in the yard. "She's getting it!" Burke called encouragingly.

Wenling was panting. She ran up to Cooper and Burke, and of course I was right beside her.

"All right!" Burke said. "That went really well."

Winded, Wenling nodded.

"Ready for the acid test?" Burke challenged.

Wenling nodded again.

"Cooper!" Burke called. "Okay!"

Before I could react, Cooper jumped playfully on my back, then turned and dashed away, daring me to pursue. I went after him, and while I scrambled to catch him, he cut to one side, and, once again, I remembered swimming in the pond. A sudden turn had made me swallow water and lose the ball, but a wide, sweeping arc had kept my head dry. And just now, running around and around with Wenling, we'd again taken wide turns, and I'd been able to run with her without dumping the cart.

It was actually less of a conclusion than an instinct. I knew how to play Tip the Cart—I'd become something of an expert at it. And this was the opposite! I now understood how to run without playing Tip the Cart.

To catch Cooper, I needed the cart to stay upright. So that's what I did.

"Lacey! You're such a good girl!" Wenling praised.

Later, ZZ and Mom came out to watch me chase my best dog friend around the yard. As long as I didn't allow the cart to fall over, I was able to keep up with Cooper easily.

"See, Dad? Lacey gets to play like a normal dog now."

ZZ nodded. "You did a good job training her."

"She was stuck. So I got her unstuck," Wenling explained simply, grinning at Mom.

I played and played with Cooper until we were both exhausted. We drank water and lolled in the shade. When I folded my front legs under me, it was fairly comfortable, though I liked it better when Wenling unfastened my straps and let me lie with my stomach in the stiff grass.

We both looked up lazily when ZZ came out through the new gate and up to us. "I want to show you something I did in the backyard," he told Wenling and Burke.

"Cooper, Pull," Burke commanded. Instantly, we were all looking at Cooper, who snapped into one of his moods. Cooper strained at the leash that ran to Burke's chair, and Burke pushed on his wheels with his hands, and we all moved together into the backyard.

"You built a ramp!" Wenling exclaimed.

Wenling led me over to the back steps, but they were missing. In their place instead was a smooth row of boards leading from the ground to the back porch. I sniffed at them curiously, noting the tang of new, clean wood.

Wenling walked to the top of what was once the steps and stood on the porch. She clapped her hands. "Come, Lacey," she called. I looked at her. I knew what *Come* meant, and often there was a treat involved, so I felt like obeying. But she was up there, and I was down on the ground. Was I supposed to get on the porch? How could I jump up there? My back legs were still strapped down in the cart.

Wenling took two steps down and reached out. She touched me under the chin, stroking me, and I closed my eyes in pleasure. Then she hooked a finger through my collar. "Come," she repeated. This time, she started pulling me steadily as she walked backward to the top of the porch, and I followed willingly. I expected some sort of calamity—no dog had ever done anything like this before! But instead, I found myself smoothly pulling the cart up the boards. When I stood next to Wenling, everyone applauded. Well, everyone except Cooper, of course. But he was looking at me with bright eyes and wagging, and I knew he was proud of me, too.

"Let me give it a shot," Burke suggested. "Cooper, Pull." And with that, Cooper and Burke joined us at the top of what I eventually learned was called a *ramp*.

From that point on, when I needed to get into the backyard, all I needed to do was go down that ramp. Wenling no longer had to carry me out to do my business. I could do it on my own. (I wasn't able to squat any longer, but it didn't matter. The cart held me upright, my legs slightly splayed, so when I needed to go, I just went. Cooper was interested in this process and often lifted his leg in the same spot. It was very polite of him to do this.)

This new freedom was wonderful. All I needed to do was wheel myself over to the back door and someone would open it for me and out I'd go, down the ramp and into the yard, taking wide turns and galloping as fast as I'd been able to run before.

I loved the ramp! And I loved that my girl no longer asked me to tip over the cart. Thank goodness she'd gotten as tired of that game as I was.

I noticed on a cold morning, with Wenling standing at the back door behind me, that the leaves under my paws crinkled and were coated with frozen water. It had rained the day before and gotten very cold that night. I could smell, though, that the day would be clear and there would be no wind, a perfect day for play.

I thought about that. I thought about playing with Cooper. It had been several days. I thought about how much fun was to be had out in the world, and then I thought about the fact that right at this moment, the gate that ZZ had worked so hard on was yawning wide open again. I didn't know who might have left it that way, but clearly it was an invitation to a good dog like Lacey to go out into the world and explore.

When I finished peeing, I did not look at Wenling because I did not want to feel guilty. Instead, I trotted gaily toward that open gate, the wheels making a quiet murmur as they obediently followed me. This was going to be fun!

As soon as I made it through the gate, I could sense and hear Wenling as she ran across the backyard.

"Lacey!" she wailed behind me. "*Lacey!*"

I was headed down the driveway and couldn't think of any reason to look back. Wenling clearly didn't understand that I was going to find my friend Cooper, so her voice carried some distress.

"Lacey!"

I faltered.

My girl was calling me.

My girl, who had carried me in her arms for so many days, was yelling my name. She sounded sad and lonely that I was leaving.

I thought about how warm and loved I felt with Wenling, how, whenever she was home, she spent most of her time playing with me.

I had a cart and a ramp and an open gate. I could go out into the world again, taking wide turns. I was far enough away from the house that she would never catch me.

She had not called again. I turned to look at her, and she was standing in the driveway, watching me. The joy I'd felt at the thought of running loose was replaced by an even deeper one, a deeper joy. No one loved me like Wenling. Being with her made me happier than anything else I could ever do.

I turned in a wide circle and ran back to my Wenling. I was a good dog, and she was my girl.

When snow came, Wenling went out to shovel it, and I went out to watch her, aware of the fact that I was having to pull very hard to drag my cart. When I was in the unshoveled portion of the driveway, I was so mired down I could barely move. Several times, Wenling was forced to come over to me and help me get unstuck. I didn't understand what had changed—I'd always had so much fun in the snow! Now everything took extra effort.

"You're a good dog to keep trying, Lacey, but I don't think you're going to make it through this stuff very easily. That's one of the reasons why Burke has Cooper. Cooper pulls Burke whenever there's even a little bit of snow on the ground. It's the only way he can really move."

I didn't really understand anything she'd just said, but I had heard Burke and Cooper mentioned and hoped that meant they would soon be coming over. Cooper and I have special games we play in the snow.

Actually, the games are pretty much the same as on dry land, or the pond, but playing them in the snow makes them special.

Cooper didn't come over that day, but it wasn't long before he did. This time, Cooper and Burke were driven by Burke's brother, Grant, who sat atop a machine I had learned was called the *tractor*. It was a big old truck that moved very slowly, had huge wheels, and made a lot of noise as it rattled and bumped along.

Behind the tractor was a flat piece of wood that Grant was dragging in the snow. Burke and Cooper were sitting on this flat platform as it pulled up the driveway. Burke's chair was lying folded in front of him.

Cooper wasn't at all glad to see me at first. Then Burke said, "Okay," and Cooper remembered to be happy, jumping off the flat wood and into the snow. I bowed, but when Cooper dashed off, kicking up snow from his paws, I didn't pursue. My cart was just too heavy in the snow.

"I thought you were kidding when you told me Grant was going to drive you. Hi, Grant," Wenling said.

"Hi, Wenling. I'm allowed to drive farm equipment on the roads," Grant explained. "Don't need a license for that." He turned to his brother. "Should I leave your chair down here next to the house?"

"That would be great, thanks," Burke replied. Grant climbed down and unstrapped Burke's chair and leaned it up against the house, still folded up.

"Cooper was not happy sitting on the toboggan with me," Burke added. "He wanted to pull me instead."

"I have no idea how Lacey will react," Wenling replied.

Cooper and I had heard our names and were watching our people to see if they wanted us to do something. They did. Wenling sat on the thin wooden platform and called to me, and, when I approached, she held my cart and guided me to stand in front of her. Burke was already there, sitting in front of both of us.

With a lurch, the tractor hauled us through the snow and up the long, long hill behind the house. Cooper galumphed alongside us, leaping forward and up with every step. His tongue was lolling, and his jaw was relaxed. Cooper loved the snow more than any dog I knew.

"Let me know when it's far enough!" Grant yelled over the loud thunder of the tractor.

"Thanks," Burke replied, "I think this will do it right here."

The tractor rattled and then quit. The silence felt strange and muffled after all the racket. Grant jumped down, his boots crunching in the snow. He untied the leashes that held the wooden platform to the tractor. "I'll get you turned around."

"I'll help," Wenling offered. I watched uneasily as she stood up and pushed on the back end of the platform. I didn't really like the jerky way the platform moved when it was shoved, and I wished Wenling could come back and sit on it with me.

With Wenling's efforts and Grant pulling on the leashes, we were spun around until we faced downhill. Cooper was wagging. I wondered if he understood what was going on, but decided that was impossible. This was well beyond the comprehension of any dog.

Sometimes all a dog can do is accept what people are doing and wait for them to do something else.

8

"So there you go," Grant declared. "Stick to where the tractor tires packed the snow down. That'll be the easiest going for you."

"Thanks," Burke sang out. He sounded excited, and I noticed that Cooper picked up on this, his ears going back playfully.

"You don't want to stay and sled with us?" Wenling wanted to know.

Grant shook his head. "I'm going to put the blade on the tractor and clear the snow off the pond so we can ice-skate. Got some friends coming over."

With a wave, Grant climbed up on the tractor, and the thing bellowed back to life. He just liked to drive places slowly and loudly, I decided. I preferred ZZ's truck.

As Grant trundled off, Burke turned and raised his

eyebrows at my girl. "You sure you wouldn't rather go ice-skate with the other kids? I don't mind."

Wenling shook her head. "I want to hang with you. This'll be fun. I love to sled."

"Just seems like you and Grant should talk about things."

"Let's not go there, Burke."

Burke sighed. "Okay."

In this case, *Okay* had no meaning for Cooper, who heard the word without reacting.

Wenling took me out of my cart and set it aside in the snow. Burke and I were both on the platform still. He was near the curved front end, and I was right behind him.

Wenling crunched around in back of us.

"You ready?" she asked. I realized she was standing in the snow, bent over, her hands on the rear of the flat board.

"Ready," Burke replied.

"Stay out of the trees."

"Would you just push the sled? I know how to toboggan."

Wenling laughed. The people seemed excited. Cooper and I glanced at each other. We were ready to be excited, too, as soon as we figured out what was going on.

"Here we go!" Wenling shouted. She gave a few grunts, and I could hear her running behind us. Cooper began bounding through the deep snow, trying to keep pace as we gathered speed. With a thud, my girl landed behind me, reaching up and gathering me in both arms.

It was like a car ride on a piece of wood! We bounced and jounced down the hill, sliding and turning and tipping. Wenling was laughing, and Cooper was right beside me, leaping powerfully. When we finally came to a halt, we all just lay there, panting in exhilaration. I briefly closed my eyes, loving the sensation of being held by my girl. Then Cooper was on top of me in a spray of snow.

"Cooper!" Wenling laughed, spluttering. She reached out, and Cooper let her roll him in the snow even though he was almost as big as she was. Then he dashed around and around us, biting at the snow in sheer joy.

I knew I couldn't run around with Cooper, not anymore. But I wanted to.

"Okay, now, let's see if this part works," Burke said. He hooked leashes up to Cooper's harness. "Cooper's a malamute—that's a kind of sled dog—so it shouldn't bother him to be pulling a sled instead of me in my chair."

I was hearing *sled* enough to conclude that was the name of the flat board that we could ride like a car.

"Cooper," Burke said softly.

Cooper instantly forgot how to be a dog and stood stiffly, entirely focused on his boy. He waited patiently

as Burke took Cooper's leashes and tied them to the curved front of the sled.

I whined. I could tell something special was happening, and now that Wenling was no longer holding me, it wasn't fun to be lying in the sled.

Wenling spoke up. "Let's see what Lacey does. In the snow, I mean. It's as slippery as the floor, and it won't hurt her tummy."

Burke thought about it. "Okay."

Wenling carried me to lie next to Cooper. The snow felt cool on my stomach. I had been spending so much time in the cart lately that it felt strange to be without it. Just about the only times I was separate from the cart these days was at night, when I lay across Wenling's bed.

Cooper was still in one of his moods, practically motionless. I panted at him, demonstrating how a *fun* dog behaved.

Wenling was behind me, sitting on the sled. "I can push if we need me to," she offered.

"Let's just see if the dog can do it," Burke suggested. "You ready, Cooper? Pull!"

With a determined look on his face, Cooper lunged forward, straining at his leashes. After a moment, the sled began moving away from me.

I was absolutely bewildered.

Both Wenling and Burke were calling my name and yelling, "Pull!" That was a command I'd heard before, but I thought it was only for Cooper. I'd never imagined it could apply to me.

Cooper dug in his claws, his head lowered, and the sled picked up speed. Wenling laughed in delight. "He's doing it!"

"The snow is nice and packed!" Burke replied.

I sat, stunned, watching the distance between me and my girl and my friend get bigger and bigger. "It will go faster if I push," Wenling said, rolling out into the snow. She jumped up and grinned at me. "Come, Lacey!"

When she bent down and pushed the sled, Cooper was able to make much quicker progress. In a near panic, I scrambled with my front legs, plowing through the heavy snow until I fell into the trough created by Grant's tires. This surface was smooth and slippery and cold and felt good on my stomach.

Burke turned and grinned. "Look at how strong Lacey is," Burke admired. "See her muscles? All that work she's been doing has really built her up. It's amazing."

"Good dog, Lacey!"

I didn't know what *Pull* meant, but I was a good dog, and soon we were all the way at the top of the hill. Wenling was panting a little, but there was a big smile on her face. "Ready to go?"

Burke was gazing at the sky. "You know, I think it's going to snow again. They're not calling for it, but that sure looks like a snow squall headed our way. See how dark the clouds are?"

"That's Michigan. Always refusing to follow the forecast," Wenling agreed cheerfully.

"I told Grant to give us a couple of hours. Don't want to get stuck out here in a blizzard."

Wenling patted her pocket. "I've got my phone if that happens."

We had so much fun going up and down, up and down, but after a while, Cooper and I were both panting.

"I think maybe the dogs need a break," Burke observed.

"Me, too," Wenling admitted. "As fun as it is going downhill, I'm starting to get really pooped coming back up."

I knew the word *poop,* but I didn't see how it applied in this situation. The four of us sprawled out contentedly in the snow. Little bits of it were starting to fall from the sky; tiny flakes that drifted lazily in circles before landing on Burke's head and Wenling's eyelashes.

"Maybe this is the last run down," Burke said. "Think between Cooper pulling and you pushing we can get from the bottom of the hill to your house?"

"Sure. This has been so fun."

"Starting to snow harder." Burke looked up at the sky.

"Oh no," Wenling said. She was frowning.

"What is it?"

"My cell phone, I can't find it."

"What? Oh, man, it must have popped out of your pocket."

Wenling rolled up onto her hands and knees, patting the snow. I watched her curiously. Sometimes when she patted the bed, she wanted me to jump up with her, but I couldn't do that anymore. And jumping didn't seem to be what she wanted now anyway. "It could be anywhere," she said mournfully.

"It's got to be somewhere along where the toboggan packed the snow," Burke told her. "Let's leave the sled here and find it."

The game changed then. Burke said, "Assist," and Cooper, of course, forgot all about what fun we'd been having. Burke reached up and grabbed the handle on Cooper's harness, and the two of them moved slowly down the hill, Burke patting the snow. Next to him, Wenling crawled along, also patting the snow.

Utterly baffled, I took slow, tedious steps forward, keeping pace, pulling myself as if it were the living room floor. We left the sled at the top of the hill and descended this way, barely moving.

Soon, the snow was falling hard enough for me to be able to hear it as it landed on the leaves and the trees.

Burke suddenly stopped. "You know what, Wenling?"

She looked at him.

"This is worse than a lost cell phone. We're out here in the woods and we've got to get back before the storm gets worse. I can barely see as it is."

"It's a blizzard," Wenling agreed. "Let's just go straight to my house. Do you want me to go back up and grab the sled?"

Burke nodded. "Yes, and then let's *go*."

The snow was so thick in the air that it coated Cooper's fur. He looked funny with the flakes all over his face and along the tips of his ears.

Wenling ran up the slippery part of the hill. Frantic that my girl was leaving me, I tried to keep up, but as soon as she reached the sled, she grabbed its leash and turned and came right back to me.

There was an urgency to everyone's movements as we got ourselves into our familiar positions on the sled. Burke wrapped his arms around me. Cooper was told, "Pull!" He lowered his head and determinedly headed downhill, while Wenling pushed from behind.

I guessed the people had gotten tired of patting the snow, which was fine by me, because as games go, it was pretty uninteresting. "If we keep heading downhill, we should eventually come to my house," Wenling said. "But if we stay in the tractor tracks, we'll miss it."

"So you think we should turn?"

"It's the only way I can think of to make sure we don't wind up going off into the fields," she answered him.

She waded through the snow and seized Cooper's leash. "This way, Cooper," she said, tugging him off the path.

The going seemed to be much tougher all of a sudden. Wenling was sinking up to the tops of her boots, while Cooper's gait slowed as he plowed the snow with his massive chest.

"Look at it snow! It just keeps falling harder," Wenling said. I looked at her because I sensed a real worry in her voice. Then she stopped. "Oh!"

"What is it?"

"I left Lacey's cart at the top of the hill. I should go get it."

"Okay," Burke agreed. "But hurry. We don't have much time before it's going to get dark."

I whimpered as Wenling turned and raced back in the direction from which we'd just come.

"Stay, Lacey," Burke told me firmly.

I still didn't know what *Stay* meant. And anyway, Burke was Cooper's person, not mine, and I belonged with my girl. I slid off the sled and sank into the deep snow.

"Lacey!" Burke called.

I ignored him, feverishly going after Wenling. She was breathing hard, which made her easy to track despite the blinding snow. I stayed on her scent, and gradually her figure emerged from the gloom. She whirled in surprise. "Lacey! What are you doing, you silly girl?"

She knelt, and I closed my eyes as she stroked my ears. "Okay, I think it's right around here. Isn't it? Did we really climb so high?" She kicked at the snow. "The tracks are filling in. I'm not sure we're still following the tractor's ruts anymore." I heard her worry breaking out into actual fear, and I lifted my head to her, trying to tell her that whatever was going on, her dog was with her.

She was peering around, blinking. Suddenly, she brightened. "There!"

We'd come back for the cart. Wenling picked me up and placed me in it. My stomach was so numb I couldn't feel the straps. "Okay, Lacey, let's take a break. I need to catch my breath."

We stood silently for several moments, the only sounds Wenling's panting and the hushed shower of the snow falling from the sky. I stood, glad to be resting. I became alert, though, when she said, "Okay," and went to the rear of the cart and started pushing it. "Pull, Lacey! Pull!"

Okay and *Pull* were Cooper words, but I decided she wanted me to head back down the hill, which was a much easier direction for me. We bumped along for a short time, and then she stopped, glancing around. "I can't see our tracks, Lacey! I don't know which way to go!"

I was startled by the alarm in her voice. "I can't leave Burke out in this snowstorm," she told me, panting. There was real dread in her words, of which I recognized one:

Burke. Then she repeated the name in a yell. "Burke! Burke!" she cried. "Can you hear me?"

She stood motionless. "Burke!" she shouted again. "Cooper!"

She turned to me and held out her trembling hands. "Oh no, Lacey."

She'd said the name *Cooper.* Did she want us to go to Cooper? I could smell him some distance away, down the hill.

We were not having fun now. And I began to think that there was one thing more important than having fun. Even more important than being loved by my girl. And that was to help her when she was distressed.

But how?

9

Fear and frustration boiled off my girl's skin—I could smell it. "Burke!" she yelled at the top of her lungs. Then she stood still, listening I listened, too, but the only sound coming to me was the constant snowfall.

The day's light was beginning to make way for gloom. I gazed up at Wenling, wondering what she needed from me. She looked down. "Okay, Lacey." Her voice was wobbly. "I need to get going. Even if I get more lost, I need to keep moving. If I just stand here, we'll both freeze. We'll go downhill, and if we find Burke and Cooper, great, and if we don't, hopefully we'll find the house and we can call for help. And if we miss the house, we might find the road, or . . ." She sighed. "Or we might wander into the fields and be lost forever." She gazed down at me, blinking the snowflakes away. "I'm so sorry, Lacey."

I couldn't bear that she was so sad. I nosed her, and she distractedly patted me on the head. "Okay, let's go," she muttered.

She walked ahead of me, pulling my leash, while I struggled to drag my cart in the snow. Usually, my cart rolled right along with me, but now it was so difficult to move. I didn't understand why.

And I didn't know why Wenling was so unhappy or how to help her. Maybe Burke would know. Or Cooper. Cooper was such a serious dog sometimes, and when he was like that, he was helping Burke. Maybe he'd know what to do to help Wenling.

It seemed like Wenling didn't think so, though. She was leading me away from our friends. I could smell them off to the side, and it just seemed wrong to leave them when we had been playing together all day. I slowed, resisting her pull. She turned and frowned at me. "What is it, Lacey?"

I leaned in the direction where I knew Cooper and Burke were.

Wenling gazed at me. Then she dropped my leash. "Are you going to Cooper and Burke? Find them, Lacey! Good dog!"

From what I gathered, I was being a good dog, and that meant I should keep doing what I was already doing.

Wenling waited until I was in front of her. Then she bent down and put her hands on my cart. Suddenly, I found walking to be much easier.

"Burke!" Wenling called. The snow erased all sounds.

The smell of Cooper grew stronger. I steadfastly pulled my cart. Then the wind swirled a blinding amount of snow from the trees, blotting out everything. It was blowing from behind me now, straight at Cooper.

I knew Cooper could smell me and, sure enough, he barked.

Wenling gasped, and we kept moving.

When their scents were so strong we seemed to be on top of them, Burke's and Cooper's forms finally appeared. They were both covered in heavy coats of snow. Cooper wagged when he saw me.

"Burke!" Wenling exclaimed. "I thought we'd never find you. We got completely lost, but Lacey knew where you were."

"I thought that was it. I yelled, but obviously you couldn't hear me."

"We need to get home, like, now," Wenling declared.

"I can't see anything in all this snow. I'm worried we'll miss the house."

"We stayed out too late," Wenling agreed. "It's going to be dark soon."

"It's dark *now*. Think Lacey's got any more pull left in her, or should we put her in the sled?"

"I think she's decided wading through the snow is her purpose."

Burke shifted himself around on the sled, and Wenling stood behind it. "Pull," Burke told Cooper, who instantly put his head down and marched forward. Wenling grunted as she got the sled moving, tugging on my leash as she did so.

I knew this game, but it was a lot easier going downhill. "I hate making you push," Burke said apologetically, looking back at Wenling struggling, her boots sinking with every step.

"Just look for lights. Do you see anything?"

"Nothing yet. I'm really worried, Wenling."

"Don't be. We'll get there," my girl answered reassuringly.

I felt as if I was acting like Cooper in one of his moods, focused grimly on pulling myself and my cart through the thick snow. Our humans were frightened, and it was our job to make them feel better. I could tell that everybody felt better when we were moving, so that was what we should do. My cart was back to being heavy, but I understood that I needed to follow my girl as she pushed the back of the sled.

"I can't believe we haven't found the house yet," Wenling muttered.

"Is anybody home?"

"My mom."

"Think she'd call somebody?"

"I don't know. I'm not sure she even knows we're missing. She might think we went with Grant to go ice-skating."

"But surely she'll call your phone, and when you don't answer, raise the alarm," Burke argued. "I mean, look at it snow."

"I need to take a break, Burke."

"Cooper. Halt!"

We stopped. Wenling stood with her hands on her hips, breathing deeply.

"I'm really sorry, Wenling."

"Nobody's fault."

"No, I mean that you're having to push. Look, why don't you leave me with the dogs and the sled. You'll make much faster time. The dogs'll keep me warm. Okay?"

Wenling stared at him. "No way that's happening," she declared flatly. "Leave you? Are you crazy?"

Burke pursed his lips, then wiped at the snow on them. "This isn't good, Wenling," he finally said softly.

Wenling turned and peered into the deepening gloom. "I know," she replied quietly. "I know that. Let's keep going." She started to push again. Cooper and I strained to make our way forward. I could see that Cooper was getting very tired, but he had the same determination I did. Something was terribly wrong, and the only thing we could do was this, help our people move the sled down the hill.

For a long time, all I could hear was dogs panting and Wenling breathing just as hard, all of it nearly smothered by falling snow. Suddenly, Burke sat up straighter. "I see something!" he announced.

Wenling stopped pushing from behind and stood and peered where Burke was pointing. "It's not my house. What is it? I can barely make it out," she complained. "Oh, wait! It's the hothouse. Wow, we really got off course."

"I didn't know you had a hothouse."

"Yeah, we don't use it. But you know what? I think we should use it now," Wenling declared. "It's shelter, and it has a heater. Come on!"

We moved forward again, and I stared ahead as a small house loomed up through the swirling snow. Wenling opened the door, and Burke asked Cooper to do Assist, and I dragged my cart through the snow to follow them.

It was very dark and quiet in this strange, one-room house. The smell of cold dirt was everywhere, along with the scent of rusted metal. A bag of something gave off a sharp, chemical tang. I saw Cooper turn his nose toward this strong odor.

Wenling fumbled along the wall, and suddenly, the room was brightly lit. I blinked. Long tables ran the length of the whole house, but I could smell there was no food up there—just dirt. These were dirt tables. I was disappointed to learn there even was such a thing.

Wenling flipped a switch. There was a loud clicking noise, and then a dusty odor blew into the air. "Heat," Wenling pronounced simply, pointing up into the far corner. "That's hooked to the gas line. We don't have to worry about freezing to death."

"Okay, then," Burke said, looking around. He sat on the floor next to me, and I took comfort from his hand on my neck. "Cooper. Okay!"

Cooper broke from his stiff mood and moved along the floor, sniffing at the musty odors.

"You've got a broken window there," Burke observed. Wenling looked up, so I did, too. In the ceiling, which was made of windows, a stream of snowflakes was falling through a missing pane. "Doesn't look like anyone's been in here in years."

Wenling nodded. "Yeah, my dad says the last thing he wants to do is come home after work and mess around in the hothouse." Wenling cocked her head and looked at the dirt. "But it would be so nice to plant things in here. Maybe grow seedlings toward the end of winter so they'd be ready to plant in the spring."

"That could be really cool," Burke agreed. "We could sell them at the farmers' market."

"This far north, planting season is so late that it's always

a race to get your crop harvested before the first freeze. Having sprouted plants would give you a real jump on it," Wenling added. She stared at Burke. "This is a *great* idea."

"You just need some seeds and, I don't know, fertilizer?"

"Let's do it."

They grinned at each other. Then Wenling came over and sat on the floor next to Burke. Cooper came over to be with us as well. Wenling got me free from the cart and gently laid me down.

A steady blast of warm air from the ticking, hissing machine up in the corner kept us from getting cold, and I grew sleepy as we pressed up against one another.

I wished the humans would remember that Cooper and I had been good dogs and get some bowls and fill them very full with dog food, but for some reason, they didn't.

"Now what do we do?" Burke asked. "Tell ghost stories? I know one about these two kids who were murdered in a hothouse."

Wenling shook her head and sighed. "I suppose it won't be long before my mom realizes we haven't come back. I'm not sure what she'll do about it, though."

"Or maybe Grant shows up with the tractor. He said he would," Burke suggested.

"Sure. Except I bet your dad won't let him drive the tractor in this blizzard."

I put my head down and was just starting to drift off

into a comfortable sleep when I heard a really loud blast of noise, whining loud and urgent and rapidly approaching. Cooper and I raised our heads at the same time, just as Wenling jumped to her feet. The walls of our little house were splashed with a bobbing light. "It's Mom!" Wenling cried as she peered out through the smudged glass.

When the machine noise abruptly quit, Wenling ran to the door and flung it open. Snow swirled in, and then Mom stepped over the threshold, smiling and stomping her feet. She hugged Wenling. "It was so smart of you to turn on the lights, honey," she said, her voice warm with praise. "When I borrowed Mr. Barger's snowmobile, I thought for sure I'd find you still playing on the hill. I got really worried when I made it to the top and couldn't see you, couldn't even find your tracks. It's really snowing hard out there."

"This wasn't our plan or anything. We sort of found our way here by accident," Wenling told Mom. "We were actually trying to make our way back to the house."

"As soon as I got to the top of the hill, I saw the glow from the hothouse, and I knew it had to be you," Mom replied. "I'm so relieved the two of you are safe."

"Me, too," Wenling agreed.

"We were just about to resort to cannibalism," Burke added.

Cooper and I glanced at the people as they laughed. We'd done it—the dogs had cheered up their people!

"Mom, Burke and I were thinking. It seems like such a waste to have this beautiful hothouse and not use it for anything."

Mom snorted. "Beautiful? All the dirty, cracked glass, the broken panes. I don't know if I'd call that beautiful. Look how the wood is rotting."

"Right, yes," Wenling agreed impatiently, "but we could fix that. I was thinking of planting maybe tomato seeds to grow seedlings. What do you think?"

Mom looked skeptically at Wenling. "I think your dad wouldn't like it."

"But, Mom—"

"We should probably get home."

"But, seriously, would it be okay?"

"I'll help," Burke volunteered.

Mom smiled. "The two of you make an unbeatable combination, but I'm telling you, ZZ won't be happy."

"Maybe if we don't mention it to him?" Wenling said hopefully.

"If you're going to start planting things, you need to tell him what you're up to, Wenling. I'm not going to deceive your father."

Burke and Wenling exchanged thoughtful looks.

10

Cooper and I sniffed curiously at the long, big, oily machine as Mom tied the sled to the back of it. Then Mom straddled the thing, and Wenling climbed up behind her mother while Burke sat in the sled, holding me. My cart was folded up in front of Burke.

With a loud roar and a lurch, the machine scooted forward, yanking the leash and pulling us behind it. Cooper didn't want to ride in the sled. He wanted to run through the snow next to us, great clouds of it kicking up under his big feet.

Mom did not go too fast, not as fast as we'd gone in the sled on the hill. I watched Cooper surging, a bit amazed at his strength, speed, and power. Cooper was a dog who was meant to run through the snow. I could see that now, the way his chest broke the powdery flakes. He could bound ahead more than the length of his own body, his strong legs lifting him completely up into the air with each jump. It was an astounding sight, and I felt lucky and privileged to have Cooper as my friend.

From that day forward, Wenling and I spent a lot of time in that strange glass house. To get there, Wenling would place my rear end in a small, scooped-out version of the sled and let me pull with my front legs while she trudged forward through the snow ahead of me, tugging a rope that was tied to my sled. It was not difficult going. In fact, when the ground dipped just before we reached what I soon learned was called the hothouse, I would sometimes speed ahead of Wenling, and she would laugh and clap her hands. "Who's the sled dog now?" she called out to me.

Unfortunately, once we arrived at the little home called the hothouse, fun time was over. I could pull myself along the wooden boards, but they were rough, and I chose instead to just nap, keeping a lazy eye on Wenling as she got busy.

She climbed a ladder and put glass over the hole in the ceiling. She swept. And then for some reason, she spent a lot of time playing with, as far as I could see, nothing but dirt.

She put dirt on the tables. She dug in it and poked

at it. She poured water into the soil that she seemed to be so fond of. None of this made any sense and was certainly less fun than swimming in the pond.

My eyes popped open one afternoon when the hot-house was filled with Mom's scent. I raised my head as she walked in the door. "With the sun out, it's nice and warm in here," she noted, looking around. "Wow, Wenling, you've really cleaned up the place."

Wenling smiled proudly. "Thanks. Lacey supervised."

I loved hearing her say my name.

Mom walked over and poked a finger into the dirt on the tables. I did not understand why everyone was so excited about getting their hands dirty all of a sudden. "You know what I think you need?"

Wenling gave her mother a questioning look.

"Compost," Mom explained.

"Like you buy in bags? I've seen it, but it's pretty expensive."

Mom shook her head. "Not that you buy, that you make. You know the piles of leaves that ZZ blew to the edge of the yard? Gather those, and some grass clippings, too. I'll give you vegetable waste from our meals. Put down straw, then the other stuff in layers. You need a layer of food waste—that's got a lot of nitrogen. And then something with a lot of carbon—like shredded newspaper, leaves, coffee grounds. Keep it moist and covered, and stir it up sometimes."

"Outside?"

"Well . . . probably better off in here, where it's a lot warmer."

I was happy to stand in my cart and watch as my girl shoveled away snow and picked up heaps of leaves, which she chopped up and threw in a pile in the corner of the hothouse. I was also happy when she collected a bucket of vegetables and eggshells and dumped it on the pile. It was just fun to be with her.

She was busily scooping things into her bucket after dinner, and I was busily waiting for her to notice there was a good dog at her side who would like very much to be involved with the cooked chicken on the counter when ZZ walked into the kitchen. Wenling stiffened.

"Wenling, what are you doing?" He stepped over and peered into her bucket.

"I'm gathering leftover salad and peas."

"Why?"

Wenling bit her lip.

"Wenling? Why are you making a bucket of these things?"

"I'm doing a compost heap."

ZZ gazed at her. "A compost heap," he repeated.

"Yes."

"A project for school?"

Wenling blinked. "It's a project, yes."

ZZ nodded. "Did you do your math?"

"Yes, all done."

"All right, then." ZZ turned away.

Wenling sighed. She focused on me after ZZ had left the kitchen. "I told the truth," she said softly to me. "It *is* a project. He was the one who said *school*."

I listened carefully, then glanced meaningfully at the chicken, which was filling the kitchen with compelling odors.

But in a few minutes, the chicken was forgotten. I watched anxiously as Wenling shrugged on a bulky coat and tromped outside without me! There was a low window in the room where people ate their people dinner, and I hurried over there anxiously, a small whine escaping my lips as my girl vanished from view, heading in the direction of the hothouse.

I could barely contain my joy when she reemerged from the gloom and came up the ramp a few minutes later, kicking snow off her boots. "Lacey, you silly! I was only gone for two minutes!" She laughed as she bent over me so I could lick her face in relief.

We went back to the hothouse the next day— together this time, which was only right. That night, after we were settled in the living room, ZZ walked into the house. He was carrying a large sack and stopped when he saw us. "Wenling."

"Hi, Dad!"

"I brought you some vegetable scraps from the restaurant. Carrot tops, scrapings from plates, rice."

Wenling stared blankly at her father, who was holding out the sack. It didn't smell very interesting.

"For your compost pile," ZZ elaborated

Wenling's face split into a big smile.

The next day, we were back in the hothouse. "These veggies add the nitrogen, and the sawdust from Dad's workshop mixes in dry carbon," Wenling told me enthusiastically. She seemed awfully excited for someone who was making a pile of what smelled like food but which, upon closer examination, actually wasn't. Some of the plant matter had obviously been near real food—I could smell traces of beef and chicken and fish—but someone had forgotten to put the good stuff in the sack.

When morning came, I was delighted to see it was one of the days when Wenling didn't say anything about school. She played with me in the snow, which was so hard-packed in the backyard I could wheel around easily. I was also able to make my way behind her down the well-traveled track to the hothouse. She flung open the door, and her shoulders slumped.

"Oh *no*," she whispered.

My nose crinkled involuntarily at the dank, strong odor of a wild creature. I could smell that it was no longer in the hothouse, but it had been inside long enough to paint its scent on many surfaces.

Wenling walked to her pile of leaves, which was much smaller than it had been the day before, and sank to her knees. "What happened, Lacey? My compost heap is all torn apart!"

I watched as Wenling dismally began gathering handfuls of plants and leaves and carrying them back to her pile. The fur was up on the back of my neck in reaction to the presence of the animal odors. And from Wenling's sadness, I could understand that whatever had been in here had upset her somehow. "How'd it get in?" she asked me.

I gazed up at her to reassure her that I loved her, in case she had forgotten.

We spent much of the day in the hothouse. My girl wanted to rebuild her pile, spraying water on it and covering it with a heavy tarp. She untied me from my cart, and I lay on the floor, drowsily watching her.

I knew something different was happening when, a few nights later, ZZ came home with another bulging sack. Like the first sack he'd brought to Wenling, it smelled teasingly of real food, but it wasn't. A mean trick to play on a good dog, I decided.

As before, Wenling totally abandoned me, vanishing out into a night that was tossing around light flakes of snow. I couldn't believe she was doing this again, and I was thrilled when she finally returned.

"You are so silly, Lacey!"

The sack wasn't the different thing about that night, and neither was Wenling's trip to the hothouse. What *was* different was that Wenling carried an odd excitement with her. When she turned out the light in her room, she lay motionless in bed, staring at the ceiling, not sleeping. I slept for both of us.

I was instantly awake when, after some time, she sat up. "Okay, Lacey."

I interpreted this *Okay* to mean that something was happening, something that had my girl excited. In a way, it was like Burke's Okay to Cooper.

Wenling dressed and put me in my cart. She grabbed something out of her closet—big and bulky—and scooped up the pillow from her bed. Then we moved noiselessly through the house and out the back door into the night.

This had never happened before. It was so much fun! I was quivering with excitement, even when it became obvious that we were going to the hothouse, where we'd already spent enough of our time. At least that's what I thought.

"Okay, Lacey. We're going to guard the compost heap," Wenling whispered. I heard my name, and I was happy.

Wenling unrolled the bulky thing and put the pillow at one end of it. Then she unstrapped me from my cart. "If that raccoon comes back, you let me know, and we'll scare it off," she whispered. "You lie on top of the sleeping bag, okay, Lacey?"

She wrestled her way inside what had once been a bundle and now looked like blankets, and she patted the soft material. With a sigh, I curled up next to my girl, feeling her warmth through the covers.

"A little cold out here," she muttered sleepily.

I awoke, the fur up on my neck, the instant I saw a shadow slinking along the glass outside. A low growl rumbled my chest as I watched the shadow scale up the side of the hothouse and reach for the window latch. With a scratching sound, the glass pressed open, and a dark face with black eyes peered around for a moment.

I knew the scent from earlier—this was the animal that had upset my Wenling! The moment it slithered inside and dropped to the floor, I was in full voice. My outraged barking made Wenling sit upright. "Lacey!"

I kept barking and dragged myself toward the startled creature. Wenling sprang to her feet and waved something that threw off a beam of light. The animal's eyes glowed. It sprang to the wall and hastily climbed straight up, lifting the window and vanishing out through the gap.

"Okay, Lacey. You did it! You scared away the raccoon. You can stop barking!" Wenling told me.

I felt pretty sure she wanted me to continue to bark until the animal's scent faded from the air. The light in her hand went out. "Okay! Enough!"

This Okay probably meant "Keep barking!"

"Lacey!" Wenling bent over and, with a grunt, hoisted me into the air. I was instantly silent—no self-respecting dog would ever bark while being held off the ground. "Good dog!"

I loved that I was a good dog, and I loved being held to Wenling's chest.

"Let's try to go back to sleep. It might come back. In the morning, I'll figure out a way to lock all the windows," Wenling whispered.

We went back to the blankets on the floor. Before we could settle down, however, a white flash of light swept across the glass walls. Soon, a bright spot of illumination was bobbing along out in the snow.

Someone was coming.

"Uh-oh," Wenling murmured.

11

A large shadow loomed at the door to the hot-house. I didn't bark, because I could smell that it was ZZ. He pushed the door open, patted the wall, and then the place was filled with light. He squinted. "Wenling?"

"Yes, Dad."

"What are you doing here? What's with all the barking?"

"The raccoon figured out how to open the windows and came in and ate all the vegetables in the compost heap," Wenling explained in a rush. "So Lacey and I decided to sleep out here to stand guard. It came in, and Lacey scared it away!"

ZZ blinked at her. "It's very late," he observed.

"I don't have school tomorrow."

He gazed at her thoughtfully. "I'll get some twine, and we'll tie the windows shut," he finally said.

I didn't understand why he left and I didn't understand why he came back, but soon, he and Wenling were playing with string while I sprawled on the blanket and wished everyone would just come over and lie down with me. "Okay. It won't get in now," ZZ grunted.

"Thank you, Daddy."

"Time for bed."

We trooped back to the house, and I gratefully sank into the blankets on the real bed. Wenling put her arms around me. "You're a hero, Lacey."

Some days later, we went to visit Cooper! "Happy Thanksgiving," everyone kept saying enthusiastically, which meant, I supposed, that they were as tantalized by all the amazing odors as I was.

The people sat around the table where all the marvelous smells were strongest. Cooper, after an Okay from Burke, sat by the table, too, his eyes burning. I had to keep licking my lips. Grant and Wenling and Burke kept letting their hands hang down near the floor. Marvelous morsels would drop from their fingers. Cooper would snap one up, and I'd wiggle on my belly to get the next one. My best friend and I gazed at each other, amazed at our good fortune.

"Anyone want more pie?" Grandma kept asking. For some reason, when she said this, ZZ and Chase patted their stomachs.

Grant always said, "Yes."

Grandma didn't play out in the yard or even leave the house much, but I was fond of her anyway. Her hands always smelled marvelous, and she usually had a treat for Cooper and me.

Even more marvelous: ZZ and Mom left after that meal, but Wenling and I spent several days at the farm, playing in the snow with Burke and Cooper and sometimes Grant. Apparently, school was over forever, because we just stayed at the farm and played. I was so happy.

Dinners were the best, because Cooper and I stood guard under the table and were rewarded with tiny handouts from the table. The people above us chewed and talked and laughed.

"Dad, did you remember to call about the dam?" Burke asked at one point.

Cooper and I glanced at each other because we picked up a whiff of discomfort from the humans.

Chase cleared his throat. "Tell you the truth, son, I clean forgot."

"All this snow melts, it's going to put a lot of pressure on the retaining wall. They really need to clean out the spillway before the spring rains hit."

"Do you ever think of normal stuff, Burke?" Grant challenged with a laugh.

"I'll make a call," Chase promised vaguely.

It didn't seem that we were going to live at Cooper's farm for the rest of our lives, though. That was all right. I was happy to go home, too, the day Mom returned and Wenling unstrapped me and placed me in the back seat of the car. As we drove away, I watched Cooper watching me.

Once home and back in my cart, I followed the track through the gate and into the backyard. I stayed right behind Wenling as she mounted the ramp. ZZ was standing there waiting for us.

"Hi, Dad!" Wenling sang.

"Welcome home," ZZ replied evenly. "Got something to show you out behind the garage."

Wenling nodded hesitantly. "Okay."

We went off track, and it was slower going through the shallow snow. I lifted my nose to the tang of clean, new wood. Off the back of the garage, I saw wire fencing and a wooden box. "Oh!" Wenling exclaimed. "It's a . . ." She looked up questioningly at her father.

ZZ nodded. "Chicken coop. With a henhouse."

"Chicken coop?" Wenling responded. She sounded excited. "We're going to get chickens?"

ZZ nodded again. "Best thing for a compost heap, chicken droppings."

"Wow."

"Not just that. You'll get eggs." ZZ regarded Wenling. "When I was a boy, it was my job to take care of the chickens. It's hard work. You have to keep them warm and clean and well fed. You can never take a day off. I'll bring home scraps from the restaurant. Chickens will eat *anything*."

"I didn't know that!"

"I've rigged the henhouse with heat on a thermostat. It's important to keep them warm, but not too warm. And I put in nesting boxes every few feet. That's so when they begin laying, they can spread out." He pointed. "See, I put ventilation holes in the top."

"Won't the ventilation holes at the top let all the warm air out, since warm air rises?"

ZZ grunted. "You would think so, but the rising air will also pull moisture with it, and that will make for a much drier coop. And that prevents frostbite and helps your chickens stay warmer."

Wenling's eyes were shining. She grinned down at me. I was happy because they were saying the word *chicken* so much. I *love* chicken.

"You can sell the eggs at the farmers' market, maybe some to the neighbors. Make a little money for yourself," ZZ concluded.

Wenling ran and gave ZZ a big hug. He put his arms

around her and hugged her back. "Okay," he said after a short while, "let's go look at your chickers."

I followed ZZ and Wenling into the garage. There was a cardboard box set on the ground, and from inside of it, I could both smell and hear tiny arimals. "Oh my, look at that!" Wenling cried out.

As I pulled my cart over to take a deeper sniff, my head just cleared the edge of the box. Inside it, scampering around aimlessly, were a bunch of small birds. There were a lot of them. I didn't understand what they were doing here, but clearly, they were astounded to see anything so wonderful as a dog, because they stared at me, moving their heads in jerky motions.

"You need to keep them here with that light bulb going for warmth, change their straw, and always lock the garage. We don't want a fox getting in." ZZ lectured.

Wenling nodded solemnly. "Can I hold one?"

"Yes."

Wenling reached down and tenderly picked up a little peeping bird. She held it for me to sniff, but I found it rather uninteresting. "Such a sweetie," Wenling murmured.

"They're called *pullets*, this age. Little more than a month old."

"Dad, thank you so much!"

ZZ grunted. "Maybe, you find out how much work goes

into taking care of chickens, you'll realize why I want you to do something else with yourself besides being a farmer."

Wenling didn't reply to this.

What I thought of as a bird was actually called a *chicken*. Not the chicken that sometimes meant "chicken treat." And not the chicken that sometimes was secretly handed to me by Wenling's little hand at the dinner table. This was a different, worthless kind of chicken, a living bird that made a lot of squawking and squabbling noises. Chickens grow very fast, and it wasn't long before they had moved out of the garage and were living in the new fenced-in area.

"Chickens are omnivores," Wenling told me. "That means they eat anything—grass, seeds, bugs. They'll eat eggshells. It's actually really important to give them eggshells so that their own eggs' shells will be strong."

When the birds were little, I had decided that they weren't very interesting. And now that they were the size of cats, they still weren't very interesting. They regarded me with utter contempt, which I felt was completely inappropriate.

I was Wenling's dog, and they were Wenling's chickens. I had my own cart—they didn't even have front legs. It seemed to me only natural that they would see me as head of the pack, but they did not.

Wenling loved those chickens, which was even more inappropriate. She spent a lot of time cleaning up after them, scooping up their poop and tossing it on the smelly heap. And when she fed them, it was with *my food*!

ZZ would come home in the evenings with two bulging bags. One of them smelled mostly of not-food—I knew all about sacks like that. But from the other sack would flow all of the most wonderful meaty odors there were. Beef and chicken and pork and cheese and shrimp and fish . . .

I was just fine with Wenling dividing the sack of not-food items between the smelly pile and the chickens. But I was outraged when the sack full of wonderful food, the one that was *obviously* for dogs, was completely emptied for the chickens as well! They attacked my food, shaking their heads, pecking because they didn't have any forepaws or even teeth, while I watched in dismay from the other side of the fence.

I remembered the gate being left open so that I could run out and explore. I began watching to see if the same thing might happen to the chickens' gate. It only needed to happen once. Let them go somewhere else.

But Wenling always very carefully checked to see that the chickens' gate was not only shut but locked.

One night, as I lay beneath Wenling's chair at the table (they were having *real* chicken on top of that table!), ZZ turned to my girl. "How is the compost project coming?"

"It's starting to give off gasses, and it's warmer than the air," Wenling replied carefully.

"Excellent. That means it's breaking down," he noted.

"Good work," Mom added.

"Thanks."

"Won't be long before you could mix it with soil," ZZ said.

Wenling didn't reply.

"Is that part of the school project? Enriching soil with it?"

Wenling cleared her throat. "I did think I should add it to soil."

There was a silence. "Wenling," ZZ said finally. "Why don't you tell me what's really going on?"

"What do you mean?" Wenling asked evasively.

"This isn't for a school project."

Wenling was silent.

"Wenling? The compost heap is not for a school project, is it?"

"Not really," Wenling replied in a small voice.

"You need to tell me everything."

Wenling took in a breath. "So, I'm going to use money from selling eggs to buy seeds and plant them in the hothouse. That way, when it's spring, I'll have plantings I can sell."

"Why did you tell me this was for school?"

Mom frowned. "You said that, Wenling?"

"*No.* I said it was a project. It *is* a project," Wenling insisted. "I never said it was for school. Burke and I are making a project of growing plantings in the hothouse."

ZZ gazed at her. "Plantings. You can already buy those at the store."

"That's true," Mom agreed from her side of the table. "But I imagine they are factory-farmed somewhere and not raised carefully by a girl who loves doing it, planted in dirt that's been composted with chicken manure."

ZZ glanced at Mom, and she smiled sunnily back.

"Plus these will be *delivered,*" Wenling added excitedly. "I'll ride my bike and take them to my customers. And I'll tell them when to plant and how to take care of their gardens, and I'll give them some homegrown compost, too."

"Why?" ZZ wanted to know. "Why do all this work?"

"So I can earn some extra money," Wenling responded simply.

"For what?" ZZ demanded suspiciously.

"ZZ, a girl Wenling's age needs money for clothes and things. Plus maybe she could save some for college," Mom explained reasonably.

"What did you think you were going to plant?" ZZ asked.

Wenling looked unhappy. "What did I *think*? Um, I don't know. I read that the most popular plants are tomatoes, cucumbers, and peppers."

ZZ frowned.

"I really want to do this," Wenling concluded softly.

Everyone was silent, and I sensed something important was being discussed.

"No," ZZ finally responded.

Wenling stared. I got the feeling that she didn't like the word *no* any more than I did.

ZZ was shaking his head. "Your first batch should be things that grow in the early spring. Like beets, carrots, radishes, celery. Then you mix in more compost, and then you plant the tomatoes and the rest. You try to put tomatoes in the ground too early and you'll not get anything."

Wenling was smiling. I guess she'd forgotten all about hearing *no*. "Thank you, Daddy."

ZZ pointed at her. "You may not fall behind in school."

"Of course not."

ZZ nodded. He glanced at Mom. "There is an important lesson here. Growing things is hard work. Then you must sell the things you've grown. If nobody wants your plantings, or if they are far cheaper at the store, you will have done all that work for nothing. That's farming."

"I understand, Dad."

"Your plan to use egg money makes sense. A lot of people wait to get their chickens until the spring, but if you do that, just as they're ready to lay eggs, around twenty, twenty-four weeks, the days start getting shorter.

And sometimes the birds'll wait all the way till the next season," ZZ observed.

"But your little guys will start laying eggs this spring, just when the days start getting longer," Mom added.

ZZ shook his head. "That might be too late, though. If you can't get seeds until you get money from those eggs, you'll miss your first crop. How about I loan you the money to order your first seeds? You can pay me back with egg money."

Wenling jumped up from her chair to hug her father and her mother and then me. I was glad we were all happy again.

Later that night, Wenling bent over me. "It's not for college, Lacey. I'm going to save the money and give it to my dad and Chase so we can keep the orchard."

12

From that day forward, as soon as the bus dropped Wenling off at the foot of the driveway, she ran up, said hello to me (I always greeted her joyously), and then we went to look at the chickens. Despite seeing both of us every single day, they always stared back as if they had no idea who we were.

I was really ready for Wenling to release those birds into the wild. Maybe she would take them down to the pond to swim with the ducks, or maybe she'd let them fly up into the trees with the crows—I didn't care. I was just tired of the smell of them, and I was jealous that Wenling gave them so much attention.

Winter turned hard, cold, and wincy, and Wenling *still* went out to the chicken house first thing in the morning, and then when she got home from school, and then again right before she went to bed. I tried to be friendly, but the one time I stuck my nose up to the wire fencing in greeting, the dumb chickens came over and started pecking at me. Clearly, they did not know how to behave around a good dog who had her own cart. I decided to ignore them.

Every day, Wenling would take the foul-smelling chicken poop out of the coop and dump it on the stinky pile in the hothouse, stirring it occasionally and then covering it with its tarp. Sometimes when she lifted that plastic, the fragrance was so powerful I wanted to roll in it, but this was not allowed.

The days were just growing longer again and the snow had stopped falling when, one day, Wenling went on one of her visits to the chickens. She climbed into the little house behind the wired fence, and then I heard her let out a huge squeal.

I was excited because she was excited, and I met her when she scrambled out of the little house and thrust open the gate. The chickens scattered in alarm.

Wenling was carrying something I couldn't smell as she dashed to the house. We both went up the ramp and inside. Mom and ZZ were sitting in the living room, staring at a flickering box on the wall, but they turned their attention to us as we burst into the room.

"Eggs!" Wenling cried out. "I've got eggs. But look!" Wenling held out her hand, and I saw that there were a couple of tiny objects cupped in her palms. They didn't smell like much of anything except maybe chickens, but not chicken. "They're so tiny! Is something wrong? They're beautiful, but I can't sell them if they're going to be this small."

"No, it will be all right. Those are called *fairy eggs*," ZZ explained. "They don't have a yolk. But don't worry. The chickens will start laying normal eggs pretty quickly."

"Fairy eggs? Is that why they're blue?" Wenling asked.

ZZ shook his head. "Your chickens are Ameraucanas. They have a virus that makes their eggs blue, but otherwise has no effect."

"They really are pretty," Mom marveled.

"Meanwhile," ZZ continued, "we need to put chipped hemp down under the straw. Otherwise, the eggs might break."

Soon, there was a new aspect to our daily visit to the obnoxious chickens. Wenling still cleaned and cleaned and talked to the birds as if they were dogs. She still took the poop to the hothouse and dumped it in the big heap covered by a tarp. But now she also took the time to carefully gather up small, nearly odorless balls in a small basket. "See the eggs, Lacey?" she'd ask.

This was as confusing to me as calling these dumb birds *chicken*. An egg is something delicious that appears in the kitchen in the morning. It sometimes has bacon or ham next to it, and a good dog will be fed some by her girl almost certainly.

Now, though, Wenling kept saying *egg* about these small, light-colored balls that she treated very gently. Even more confusingly, after we ate real eggs, Wenling would crush the fake eggs—now just shells—under her palm. Then she'd take them out and scatter them on the ground where the chickens lived. They would peck at the fragments as if eating them. "They need the calcium," Wenling told me.

I didn't know what she was saying. I didn't want to eat the flavorless pieces of these egg balls, so I ignored them. "I also give them ground-up oyster shells now, Lacey," Wenling told me. "They need it or the eggshells will be too thin and the eggs will break when they lay them."

I wondered why, if the word *egg* was going to be said so much, we didn't go inside where they were and eat a few of them.

On a day when Wenling didn't run off to the school bus at the bottom of the driveway, she took me out of my cart and climbed with me into ZZ's truck to sit with Mom. ZZ put my cart in the back, and Wenling held me as we drove to what I knew of as town.

Town is a place where the buildings and people are packed more closely together than they are at home. The normal smells of animals—both wild and those standing behind fences—vanish. Instead, I only catch whiffs of an occasional dog or a squirrel. I was prepared to chase the squirrels, but Wenling always kept me on a tight leash.

"It's the farmers' market, Lacey," Wenling told me after ZZ parked the truck and we got out of it. She was talking to me as she put me back into my cart, but she used another set of words that I did not understand, even though they were directed at me.

Rows of tables were set up with a wide aisle between them. People mingled in that aisle, along with a dog or two connected to their people with leashes. A few of the tables were stacked with treats, some sugary and some flooding the air with meat smells, but Wenling did not stop to examine these.

I was disappointed, but at least none of the tables had dirt on them like the ones in the hothouse.

"Come on, Lacey," my girl urged, pulling me forward. Then I halted. I could detect something wonderful up there on one of the tables—*real* chicken, uncooked. But my girl wouldn't let me stop there. She kept pulling me forward.

Mom and ZZ followed us, carrying big boxes. I wagged when we approached a table with Chase standing behind it. Burke was there, too, and he wheeled out to greet us. Cooper stood stiffly at his side and didn't wag at me, but I was used to such strange behavior from him.

"The nice weather's brought out a lot of people,"

Chase observed. "Been selling Grandma's canned tomatoes and asparagus like hotcakes."

"No, the guy with the pancakes is selling *those* like hotcakes," Burke corrected. "I've got canned blueberries here, which you could put *on* the hotcakes."

"I need to pick up a couple of jars of tomatoes," Mom remarked.

"I'll save them for you," Chase offered.

"Thank you for letting me share table space with you," Wenling said as she set out small boxes filled with the nearly odorless eggs—the small balls she never threw for me to chase.

"Oh, eggs!" a woman exclaimed, coming up to see me. She didn't pet me, though. Maybe seeing those balls that never got thrown had put her in a bad mood. I could understand how that could be.

"How fresh are they?" the woman went on.

"No more than two days old," Wenling replied.

I watched, befuddled, as the inedible eggs that Wenling treated so lovingly were handed over in exchange for pieces of paper and small bits of metal. This happened over and over. I could tell that Cooper didn't understand any of it, either, even if he pretended he did.

Strange things were going on, and Wenling kept paying attention to those eggs instead of me, but I still enjoyed the day because so many people made a fuss over me. I was a special dog now because I had my own cart.

None of the other dogs walking down the aisle had a cart.

As much as I wanted to romp and play with the other dogs who came wagging by, I understood that, in a way, I had to be a little bit like Cooper. Running around in this small aisle between the tables probably would not make Wenling very happy. I'd stay by her side and try to be serious, just like Cooper did with Burke.

Gradually, there were fewer and fewer people strolling past. "I'm out of eggs, Mom," Wenling declared. "Is it okay if I walk around?"

"Don't go far," Mom told her.

"Cooper. Pull," Burke commanded.

Wenling led me on leash past tables where people were handing out plants to other people There were no dog treats or any dog toys, and the woman who had been standing at the table with the delectable raw chicken smell had packed everything up and left.

"This was fun," Burke said. "Are you coming next week?"

"As long as they keep laying eggs," Wenling replied cheerfully.

"Well, my grandma said I could have the money from selling the blueberries, since I picked them. So here." Burke held out his hand. I could smell there was nothing edible in it.

Wenling stared. "What do you mean?"

"So you can buy your seeds."

Wenling looked confused.

"It's going to work," Burke told her. "We'll pool our money, and when our dads really need it, we'll hand it over."

"Thank you, Burke. My dad already loaned me money for seeds, though—I ordered them a few days ago."

Burke shrugged. "Still. We're doing it. We're saving money so they don't have to cut down the orchard. Together, Wenling—we said we're doing it together."

They smiled at each other.

We were still moving slowly, Cooper focused on taking careful steps as he tugged on his leash. It made me want to dash around the tables just to irritate him.

We halted before one table at the far end. A heavy man with fur on his face grinned at Burke and Wenling.

"Look, it's brandy with an apple in the bottle!" Burke exclaimed. I glanced at him alertly because of his excitement. From Cooper, not so much as a flicker.

"Apple brandy," the furry-faced man told Burke.

"How did you get the pears and apples into the bottles?" Wenling wondered.

The man smiled, his teeth shining in his bushy face. "Well, now, if I'm telling you that, I'm giving away all my secrets."

Wenling was touching some glass objects. I decided I wouldn't like it if she threw one for me to chase—they would be hard to hold in my mouth. "And everything you sell with the whole fruit in it is more than twice as much as your bottles without," Wenling observed thoughtfully.

The man nodded and winked. "That's the beautiful truth of it."

"Does it taste different with the apple in it?" Burke wanted to know.

The man chuckled. "Well, now, it's brandy. And I can't be serving brandy to someone as young as you two. But I'm here to tell you"—he leaned forward conspiratorially—"there's not a difference to it at all. People just pay a lot more for a bottle that has fruit in it, and there you go. It's brandy just the same, both bottles."

"Did you somehow make a bottle around the fruit?" Wenling guessed. "Like, you blow your own glass?"

The man smiled again. "You go on now, before you figure everything out. I can tell the both of you are pretty smart."

We walked away from the big, furry man. "He gets all that money just for having fruit inside the bottles," Wenling said thoughtfully.

"Right," Burke agreed. "But how does he get it in there in the first place? The neck of the bottle is way too small. You try to jam an apple in there, you won't have apple brandy, you'll have *applesauce* brandy."

"You heard him. He said we're both pretty smart. I'll bet we can figure it out."

"Are you thinking we're going to go into the brandy business?" Burke teased.

Wenling laughed.

The sun seemed particularly strong inside the hothouse for some reason, warming the air enough to make me pant. The pile of dirt and plants and chicken poop in the corner gave off an odor so strong I kept trying to climb on it, and Wenling would say that word *no* I disliked so much, and I'd have to leave it alone. Not for long, though. Soon, I'd be right back there as if pulled by a leash. That heap just needed a good dog to roll in it.

Finally, Wenling unstrapped me from my cart, set me on the floor, and tied me to one of the long tables.

Then *she* went to play in the smelly dirt! That was very unfair. Like anyone with any sense. I would rather be a dog than a person. But as I panted and watched Wenling, I had to admit that there were some ways in which being a person would be very nice. Like bacon. And pungent dirt.

Bewildered, I watched as Wenling took small amounts of the smelly dirt and carefully put it on top of the long tables.

"Every seed gets a spoonful of compost mixed in the soil," Wenling told me. I gazed at her so she would know that I was listening, though I heard no words I recognized and certainly no mention of bacon.

She used a hose so that the odors would be even stronger, spraying a mist over the tabletops. I was glad my girl was taking such an interest in the wonderful stink but felt that if she wasn't going to roll in it, she was really missing the point.

"Okay," she told me. "Carrots are in. Celery, turnips, and beets. I'll plant radishes tomorrow. Oh, Lacey, this is going to be so much fun." I picked up the happy note in her voice and hoped that whatever was going on meant we'd stop being so fascinated with the chickens, who squabbled with each other and pecked like mad at whatever Wenling tossed into their big cage, including the meat treats that should have been given to a wonderful dog in a cart.

But no, we went straight from the hothouse to the chicken yard. Wenling climbed into the birdhouse and came out with eggs. "Lacey!" She greeted me with excitement in her voice. "I just had the best idea!"

13

It took me a while, but over the years, I'd learned not to become anxious whenever the big school bus pulled to the end of our driveway and Wenling raced out the door in the morning. I knew she would be gone for what would seem an impossibly long time, but eventually, she would always return to me. Wenling was my girl and wasn't about to leave her dog alone forever.

It was different, however, the day that ZZ drove off in this truck, the melting snow making a wet, slushy sound under his wheels. Then a little while later, Wenling and Mom left in Mom's car. This had happened before—in fact, I was alone all day most days—but that didn't mean I liked it.

I could count on the school bus, which arrived and departed on such a regular basis that I could sense it even before I heard or smelled it. But when Mom or ZZ was driving, there was no telling how long I would be without my girl.

I paced anxiously, even going so far as to put my front paw up on a window ledge and look out the side window where the chickens lived. They were busy doing chicken things because they weren't bright enough to do dog things.

I barked in relief when I heard the familiar sound of Mom's car coming back up the driveway. I could hear doors shutting, and then Wenling cried out, "Lacey!"

I trotted expectantly to the back door. Even though her voice had come from the front yard, I had learned that Wenling only let me outside through the door at the top of the ramp. When she opened it, I was so excited to see her. We were back together!

She led me down the ramp, and she was excited, too—I could smell it, popping off her skin. "I can't wait to show you what I got you," she told me. We passed through the gate. Next to the car was something new. Was this the source of all the enthusiasm? It didn't look particularly special to me, but then again, Wenling was a person who could get excited about chickens or about a table covered in dirt.

I could see that the thing had wheels and was otherwise basically a flat variation of the cart that I kept under my rear legs. It reminded me a bit of the sled—just a shorter, wider sled with wheels.

"It's a two-wheeled trailer, Lacey. See? I can stack things on it, and it attaches to the back of your cart. Okay? I want to see if this works." I heard the eagerness in her voice and licked her hand in support. She fumbled around with my cart. I could feel it making small movements. Then she stood back. "Okay, Lacey!" She took my collar. "Let's go for a walk down the driveway and back."

Walk! It was strange, though, that she was clutching my collar and not leading me on a leash. I strode with her down the driveway. My front paws were having to work a little harder to pull, for some reason.

"It works," she breathed happily.

I smelled Mom coming out of the house, and when we turned in a wide circle and went back up the driveway, she was waiting for us, smiling.

"Perfect," Mom praised.

"I know! She can pull the trailer behind her cart, no problem!" Wenling exclaimed. "Now Lacey can help me deliver eggs. I'll be able to get more customers because I can go farther than when I had to keep coming back on my bicycle to pick up more eggs."

"Plus no more broken ones," Mom suggested.

"Exactly!" Wenling was beaming.

"And when you're ready to deliver your seedlings . . ." Mom seemed to be thinking.

Wenling nodded. "I'll put those on Lacey's trailer, too!"

"What did you decide to plant?"

"My first harvest will be seventy-five each of carrots, beets, radishes, and celery."

"I'm proud of you, Wenling. Between the chickens and the hothouse, you've been working so hard. Just . . ."

"Just what?"

"Just don't fall behind on your schoolwork. Your dad and I want that to always be your top priority."

"I won't!"

Mom and Wenling were both smiling, but they weren't looking at me, so I didn't get my hopes up. Sometimes people are very happy when they talk to each other, but that doesn't necessarily mean it will result in any sort of treat.

A little while later, I twisted to watch Wenling put a box on the sled with wheels, which I was starting to understand was called a *trailer*. "Let's go deliver eggs, Lacey!"

We took a walk, which was wonderful, but Wenling kept my leash tight, which was less so. We went a short distance—I could still smell the house and Mom and the chickens—and up a driveway. Wenling knocked on the door, and when it was opened, I picked up the scent of a cat.

"Hello, Mr. Barger! I've got your eggs."

A tall man with no hair on his head grinned down at me. "Look at that," he said with admiration in his voice. "That's quite the helper you've got there!"

He was grinning with so much approval I assumed a treat would be forthcoming, but instead, he handed out some dry boxes and some paper, and Wenling gave him a box in return.

We went up several driveways and then for a long walk down the road, which was wet under my feet from the melting snow. "Okay, Lacey, let's see if we can sell more eggs!"

We headed up a driveway toward a new house. I'd already smelled several cats and a few dogs along the road, so I wasn't surprised when the door that opened for us now was banged aside by a small white dog who ran to sniff my butt but was flummoxed by my cart. She came around so that we were nose to nose.

"Hi," my girl told the woman who stood in the doorway.

"Winnie! Come here!"

The white dog ignored the word *Come*, which I had long ago concluded was known to all dogs. She play bowed, and I gave her a stare back that was worthy of

Cooper. I was in a cart pulling a trailer and obviously couldn't wrestle at the moment.

"My name is Wenling Zang. I have chickens, and I'm selling their eggs."

"Winnie!" the woman said more sternly. Was she talking to me?

"Would you be interested?" Wenling pressed.

The woman blinked at Wenling. I noticed her hair was as white as her dog's, and I wondered if there was a connection. "How much are they?"

"Five dollars a dozen." Wenling opened a box to show off the odorless sky-colored balls inside. Those again! "I know that's more expensive than at the store, but these are only forty-eight hours old. Did you know that eggs can be as old as sixty *days* at the store?"

The woman frowned. "I did not know that."

The white dog squatted and then turned her back on me dismissively, passing through the open door and into the house.

"I'll take a dozen," the woman said, digging into her pocket. "How many chickens do you have?"

"Twenty-six," Wenling replied. "And when it gets a little warmer, I'll also have seedlings for sale on Lacey's trailer."

I glanced up to see if the woman knew that was my name. She smiled at me, so I guessed she did.

"Do you grow a garden?" Wenling inquired brightly.

"Oh. I have in the past, yes."

"Would you like to buy seedlings? I have carrots, beets, radishes, and celery. They'll be a collar each except for the celery, which is eight dollars. Every order comes with a free pound of compost.

"Do you have any tomato plants?"

Wenling shook her head. "It's too early for tomato plants, but that's what I'm putting in next I should have some plantings ready to go in about a month. Meanwhile, my dad says that once the soil is fifty degrees at night, you can plant. Would you like to order your seedlings now? I can't promise that I won't run out."

The woman gave Wenling an affectionate look. "I was in sales before I retired. You're a natural. Yes, I'll take a couple of each."

Cooper came to see me the next day. Burke and Wenling sat at the picnic table and talked while Cooper, who was on Okay, raced around the fence line.

I felt that Okay applied to both of us, but I wasn't in the mood to chase another dog. I'd spent the entire previous day walking right next to Wenling, pulling the trailer, while she went places to talk to people and meet their dogs. When there were no dogs, she spoke to the people anyway. Being that close to my girl gave me such a warm, happy feeling that I didn't want to break away from her.

"I'm sold out," Wenling announced proudly.

"Of your seedlings? How is that even possible?" Burke wanted to know.

"I've been taking orders when I'm out delivering eggs. Some people are even paying in advance!"

"Wow."

"I'm making more than twenty-five dollars a week on eggs now. One week, I made thirty-five."

Burke dug into his pocket. "I've been getting twenty-five every weekend to referee kids' basketball—one of the few jobs I'm allowed to do at our age. So that's another hundred dollars."

"Do you like it?"

Burke grinned. "Being a ref? I really do. The kids are hilarious, but they're so enthusiastic. It's fun watching them. The only problem is some of the fathers. They get angry if they don't like my call."

"What do you do then?"

"I'll show you. Cooper!"

Cooper instantly came to join us, all business as he sat by his person's chair.

"This is a new one. Ready? Okay. Cooper: Watch!"

Cooper snapped his cold, un-doglike eyes up to Wenling and held her in a steady glare. Wenling laughed in delight. "Wow! He really looks like he's angry."

Burke reached out a hand and stroked Cooper's forehead. "Cooper, Okay!"

Cooper turned to me, wagging.

"He's not, though. Angry, I mean. That's just Cooper. When he's working, he looks like he's mad at the world, but he's only trying to concentrate."

Wenling smiled at Burke. "I'm taking orders for peppers, tomatoes, and cucumbers next. Those are all more expensive than the early-spring crops. It's working, Burke. We're going to have the money."

Burke smiled back, and Cooper glanced at me to see if I understood that our people were happy.

The chickens seemed to enjoy the warmer weather, if a chicken can truly be said to enjoy anything. They didn't like the grass, though—they pecked it out of their yard the moment it popped up out of the ground.

I always waited impatiently for Wenling to come home from school because I knew we would take boxes of eggs and boxes of dirt and give them both to the neighbors, whether they had dogs or not. We did this every day, unless it was raining. I loved being together with my girl and didn't mind pulling the trailer.

"You're so strong now, Lacey!" Wenling praised me. I heard the approval in her voice, and it was as wonderful as being fed a treat. Well, not as wonderful as a bacon treat, but as wonderful as almost every other kind of treat.

The best days were the ones when I saw Cooper. Some days he came to visit, and some days we went to the farm to play.

One day, we were sitting on the farm's front porch and eating some of Grandma's pie, except the dogs hadn't yet been given any. I was staring at Wenling to let her know she should hand over a bite, but she was talking to Burke and ignoring me.

People do that—they get focused on each other instead of their dogs. There is nothing a dog can do about it except maybe just whine a little. I gave that a try, and Cooper shot me a disapproving glance. He never whines, in my experience.

"Sometimes I'm so tired after delivering my eggs, I take a nap before dinner," Wenling confided to Burke. "But then I open the box in my drawer and put in the money I've collected that day, and it's all worth it."

"I made you something," Burke told her shyly. He opened a folder and handed Wenling a small sheet of paper.

"You drew the orchard! It's really good, Burke!"

"I thought you could laminate it to the lid of your money box. Remind you why we're doing this."

"It's perfect," she breathed, her eyes shining.

"Want to go up there now and see the trees? They're just starting to bud out. Soon, they'll be in full flower."

"Yes!"

Cooper and I glanced over because ZZ and Chase and Grant had emerged from the barn. They were talking and laughing as they came across the field. Grant came the long way up the ramp, but ZZ and Chase mounted the steps, their boots making vibrations I could feel in my front paws.

"I heard a rumor of pie," Chase drawled. He dropped into a chair next to Burke. "ZZ, you want pie?"

"Yes."

"I'll get it," Grant volunteered. He passed into the house.

"Day like this, wind in the trees, sun shining, I don't think I'd want any other job in the world," Chase observed cheerfully.

ZZ grunted.

"Well, okay, a job where I made better money, maybe," Chase corrected himself with a nod He focused in on ZZ. "Got a question for you, ZZ. We're going to get pretty busy soon. You think we should cut down the orchard now? Maybe tomorrow?"

14

Wenling stiffened and gave Burke an alarmed stare.

ZZ seemed to be considering whatever Chase had just said. "Busy now," he finally answered.

"True enough."

Grant came back carrying a tray with plates on it. "One of those slices looks a lot larger than the others," Chase observed.

"Oh, man. You're right. Sorry. I'll eat that one," Grant replied. He handed over plates, and the air was even more full of the sweet smell of the food. I pondered whether another whine was called for.

"But why cut the trees at all?" Wenling demanded. "The orchard is so beautiful!"

Chase blinked at her, and ZZ frowned.

"Well, Wenling," Chase responded slowly, "you're right, it's beautiful. But with the cider mill up the hill shut down, we don't have any kind of market for the fruit this year. The baby food company is offering even less, barely enough money to cover the gas to drive the truck to their factory. It's just what happens in farming. Good years, bad years, worse years."

"But you don't harvest until fall," Wenling argued. "Maybe prices will go up by then. Or I could help. I could add apples and pears to my deliveries!"

There was a short silence. Chase gave Wenling a kind smile. "That's really nice, Wenling. But your dad and I got an offer for twelve hundred dollars for the wood, as long as he and I cut it and stack it. People chip apple-wood for smokers; guess that's all the rage now. That kind of money goes a long way when you're running an operation like this one."

"It's not the trees' fault!" Wenling protested.

"Wenling," ZZ warned.

Wenling looked down, biting her lip. The pie forgotten, I raised my nose to my girl, trying to give her comfort—comfort she obviously needed.

"We fit it in when we can," ZZ suggested. "Maybe cut them down in July, let the wood dry out."

"Two months from now," Chase agreed with a nod. "Don't want to let it go much longer than that."

Burke and Wenling exchanged desperate glances.

Burke cleared his throat. "Tell you what, Wenling. Why don't we go up and look at the orchard now? It *is* beautiful," Burke suggested.

Chase gave Burke a bleak look. "Son, this is a working farm, not a nature preserve. We can't keep something around just because it's nice to look at."

Burke didn't answer.

Cooper and I took our people for a walk. Cooper charged ahead, pulling his leash, while I kept pace at Wenling's side. Without the trailer, the going was very easy, even on the rutted trail beneath our feet. Everywhere, grass was full and lush, because here there were no chickens.

"Will we have the money by July?" Burke asked. He sounded worried.

"I don't know," Wenling replied, anguished. "Close, but I don't think so."

"I asked to ref more games, but so far nobody's assigned me any," Burke told her with a sigh. They were quiet for a little while. I kept eyeing Cooper, but he was pulling determinedly at the end of his leash and not even glancing at me.

"We can't let them cut down the orchard," Wenling moaned. "It's my favorite place on the farm."

"Mine, too."

"I want to do this! I hate that we're not old enough to get real jobs. Isn't that what farm families do, everyone working for the common good? Why do they make it so hard?"

"I'm not even sure our dads will take our money. They're sort of strange that way."

"That's not fair! We're trying to help!"

"Grant's able to work as a farmhand now," Burke agreed. "Dad takes *his* money. I don't see the difference."

We eventually made our way to a place on the hill where the trees were set out in row after row after row. "Look how beautiful they are," Wenling breathed.

"I love it when they blossom. Did you know the apple is the Michigan state flower?"

"No! But I get why." She turned to Burke. "Is it okay with you if I climb up there?"

"I don't mind at all. Want me to join you?"

Wenling raised her eyebrows.

"Legs aren't strictly necessary for tree climbing," Burke explained.

"Do you want to?"

Burke gazed at the treetops, then looked around. "No, I like it here in the shade. You go ahead."

"You stay, Lacey," Wenling told me. *Stay* is a word I hear a lot in my life. I have no idea what it means (except maybe "don't have fun"), but I do know I'm never happy to hear it.

155

Grunting, Wenling began climbing up into the tree. It shook as she stepped on the limbs. I watched anxiously. Even without a cart, I'd never had much success scaling trees. Now my girl was headed up there without me. I glanced around, but I didn't see a squirrel. What was the point of climbing up a tree if there wasn't even a squirrel in it?

"Don't go too high," Burke warned.

"I'm fine. I'm just looking at these buds. They're all going to grow to be pears."

"Probably will be a great crop this year. That's usually what happens," Burke observed. "Whenever the price goes down, everybody has lots to sell. You watch, we'll cut down our trees and other people will, too, now that the mill is closed. So then there won't be enough fruit, and prices will go up, and everyone will start planting again."

"Aren't there other cider mills?"

"I guess so," Burke said thoughtfully. "But they're too far away. Price of gas, doesn't make sense to drive there. Can you see the old mill from up there?"

"Yes, it looks abandoned."

"It *is* abandoned, and that's a real problem. Even more of a problem than not being able to sell to them."

"Why? What do you mean?"

"See how they put up that retaining wall to catch rain?"

"It's working. There's a pond."

"Right, because of the spring rain. But see that spill-way? That's where the water's supposed to drain out, a little at a time. But since the owners left, it's getting all clogged up with leaves and branches, so there's too much water in there. In a real downpour, the dam could burst."

Wenling drew in her breath. I looked around. Squirrel?

"If it does . . ." Burke turned and glanced back toward the farmhouse, so Cooper did, too. "It means all that water goes down the hill."

"Oh, wow," Wenling breathed. "Well, what can we do about it? Anything?"

Burke grinned up at her. "I like how you act as if you're the one who has to solve every problem for everybody. You're going to be a CEO of something someday."

"One of my egg customers says I should be in sales. But I just want to be a farmer."

Burke's grin faded. "I don't know what we can do. I don't know what *anybody* can do. I talked to Dad about it, but he said he hasn't been able to reach anyone since the mill closed."

"I remember you talking about it before, but now I get it. Is there maybe a state agency we could call?"

"I don't know."

Wenling was straining to get something from the far

end of one of the limbs. "This branch is dead," she explained.

"Hey, be careful."

Just then, my girl tumbled from the tree in a shower of sticks. She and Burke both shouted, and I jumped to my feet and barked.

Wenling hit the ground. All her air left her lungs in a gasp.

"Wenling!" Burke cried. "Cooper, Pull!"

I got to her first. I frantically licked her face. There were tears in her eyes, and she was gritting her teeth.

"My leg," she moaned when Burke arrived. "I think I broke my leg."

There was a lot about what happened next that I did not understand. Burke told Cooper "*Stay*," and Cooper sat. Then Burke wheeled himself down the rutted trail until he was almost out of sight. He raised his hands to his lips and began yelling.

"ZZ! Dad! ZZ! Dad!"

Eventually, I saw Grant come out of the house. He waved and headed our way.

"Cooper, Come!" Burke commanded.

Cooper had been observing everything anxiously. He had stayed with Wenling because Cooper had told him to, but I knew it made him nervous not to be with his boy when Burke was upset.

Now he galloped to Burke's side. "Pull!" I heard Burke say. Cooper dug in, and Burke's chair trundled quickly back to us.

"Hey. How are you doing?" Burke asked Wenling.

She shook her head. I licked her face some more, which I knew would help. I could feel the pain in her, taste it on her skin.

Grant trotted up to us, looking concerned. "What's going on?"

"Wenling fell out of the tree. She might have broken her leg."

"Oh, man." Grant looked down at her. "ZZ and Dad went to town. They should be back soon." Grant thought about it. "I'll get the tractor up here. We'll load Wenling on the tractor and take her down to the house. Then we'll call somebody."

Wenling nodded. Grant ran toward the house. I looked at Cooper to see what to do. Cooper was looking at Burke, every muscle tense.

"Okay, Cooper," Burke said softly.

Cooper nosed me, and I nibbled gently on one of his ears, but I didn't feel like playing. It seemed that we were all doing Stay, and it still wasn't any fun at all. But we did it until Grant came grinding up the rutted path in the slow-moving tractor.

Wenling put her arms around Grant, and he lifted her off the ground. As I watched this, it occurred to me that Grant and Wenling used to do this kind of thing a lot more in the past than they did now. People call it *hugging*.

My girl was holding one leg up in an awkward position. Grant grunted as he helped her climb up on the back of the tractor. She sat down facing us.

"Go slowly," she urged Grant.

When that tractor began moving, bouncing on the rutted path, I saw my girl's face twist up in pain. I followed anxiously.

"Good dog," Wenling told me. Her voice sounded as if her teeth were clenched tight.

Burke said, "Pull," Cooper dug his paws into the dirt, and Burke's chair was in the rear, following us as we made our way very slowly down the hill.

"It's okay, Lacey," Wenling kept saying. I did not know what she was trying to tell me, but I could sense that she was hurting, and I wanted to do something to make the pain go away. I thought about trying to jump up with her, but I had gotten used to having the cart behind me. I knew jumping probably wouldn't work and the cart would tip over.

By the time we arrived at the bottom of the hill, ZZ and Chase were pulling up the driveway in a truck.

"Wenling!" ZZ shouted. He ran up to us and put his

arms around her. I smelled the tears on her face and saw them leaking silently from her eyes.

"It hurts," she murmured.

"She fell out of a tree," Burke informed ZZ.

ZZ picked up Wenling and carried her so tenderly, it reminded me of before I had the cart, when Wenling would gather me gently in her arms and take me into the yard to do my business. He helped her into his truck, and I followed, naturally believing I'd go with them.

"I've got Lacey," Burke advised, reaching out and snagging my collar. "You'll be okay, Wenling."

"Thanks, Burke," Wenling replied in a small voice.

I watched, alarmed, as she drove away in ZZ's truck. No! My girl was *hurt*. She needed me! I tugged at my collar and whined, looking up at Burke expectantly. Burke would realize that I needed to go with my girl.

But he didn't. Instead, Chase loaded me, Burke, and Cooper into his truck. I recognized from the smells where we were going—home. When we arrived, Mom was standing in the front yard. She nodded as Chase got out of the car.

"Her ankle's broken," Mom informed us. "It's a clean break, though. They think it will heal fine. They're going to set it in a cast. Do you know what happened?"

Chase nodded. "The kids were climbing trees. Well, Wenling was climbing a tree, and I guess she fell. Just an unlucky accident."

I was led around the back by Mom and up the ramp and into the house. I took up position by the front window, staring out anxiously. This had never happened before—my girl getting a tractor ride while she was hurt and sad, and then getting in the car and going away from me just when she needed me most. I wanted her to come back so that everything would be normal again.

I yipped with excitement when ZZ's truck pulled into the driveway. Wenling stepped out. She was hopping on one foot, and she carried two sticks, which she shoved up under her arms. Then she made her way to the house, wobbling. I was there at the front door to greet her.

"Down, down. Stay down," she told me. I wasn't sure what that meant. I tried to put my paws on her leg, I tried to sniff at the weird heavy boot she wore on one foot, and I followed her anxiously as she made her way awkwardly to the couch and sat down with a groan.

"Does it hurt?" Mom wanted to know.

Wenling nodded. "A little. Mostly, it's just stupid."

"How long will the cast have to be on?"

"A couple of months. She'll get a walking cast in a few weeks," ZZ replied.

I went to Wenling and put my head in her lap to let her know that I forgave her for leaving me but that I really didn't want it to happen again.

At dinner that night, my girl sat with one leg sticking straight out from her, sort of at an angle to the table.

"How am I going to deliver my eggs and take care of my summer seedlings? I've already sold all the peppers and tomatoes. People are counting on them!"

There was a long silence.

"I have to work," ZZ finally said.

"Me, too, Wenling," Mom agreed. "I can't drive you."

"But, Mom!" I could sense my girl's distress. "I have to be able to deliver to my customers! They're counting on me!"

15

The anguish in Wenling's voice silenced her parents for a long moment.

"Honey, sometimes accidents happen and life has to be rearranged around the consequences," Mom finally explained sympathetically.

"Spend time to study," ZZ added.

Wenling put her face in her hands.

Since Wenling couldn't walk well with that funny, heavy boot on her foot, ZZ went out to take care of the chickens. He did so silently, his head down, and I did not get the feeling that he was happy.

I wondered why we couldn't just open the back gate and let the chickens run off. That seemed to me to be the best solution. They certainly wanted to get out. They were always rushing over to the fence whenever I came near. Then they would stare at me and move their heads in quick, jerky motions. As far as I could tell, those motions meant that they didn't understand why I was outside the fence and they were on the inside, because they were too dumb to realize that Wenling knew a dog was a far better companion than a chicken.

Wenling liked playing with her long sticks. She didn't chew them, though, which is what sticks are for. Instead, she shoved them into her armpits, and after a time, she began moving much more quickly, though with an odd, awkward gait. I followed dutifully as we went down the ramp into the backyard. She limped into the garage and called me.

I pulled my cart over to her, and she said, "Now, Lacey, I know you don't understand, but I need you to turn around. Turn around, Lacey." Wenling reached down and grabbed my collar. I allowed her to pull me so that we were both facing out the door. Then I heard her struggling with something. I wanted to help, but every time I turned to see what was going on, she told me *no*.

No was by far my least favorite word.

Eventually, I could feel my cart being jostled, and I knew she was hooking the trailer up to it. "Okay, we're going to try this." She sat down on the flat trailer. She had never done this before. "Okay, Lacey. Can you go? Can you pull? Can you go, Lacey? Go."

Well, I certainly didn't understand what we were talking about here. For a time, we just stood there, with Wenling saying things I'd never heard. Well, except for *Pull,* but that was a Cooper word that didn't apply to me.

The garage door was up, and outside there was a sweet day, with flowers and grass and leaves all jousting with each other to fill my nose. I wanted to go out there. I thought about the number of times the trailer had been hitched to my cart and how we would go for long walks to visit the neighbors and hand them plants and boring egg balls in boxes. Why didn't we do that? But we couldn't, because Wenling wasn't next to me. She was sitting on the trailer, weighing it down, preventing it from moving.

I yawned anxiously. Would it be okay for me to just step out into the sun? Wenling wouldn't like that, I reasoned, but she hadn't uttered the dreaded word *no,* so perhaps she would put up with it. I tentatively took a step forward.

"Yes! Good dog!"

These were fine things to hear. Encouraged, I strained and was rewarded by the familiar sensation of the trailer rolling behind me. It had never been this difficult, but I was able to move, and soon we were out in the sun.

"Yes! Good! Lacey, here's a treat!"

Wenling extended her stick and, balanced on the

end of it, I smelled a chicken treat. And not one for the chickens to eat but a treat made of *real* chicken. Not a dumb, feathery bird.

I was making Wenling happy. We were in the sunshine. Would she let me take a little walk? I moved forward.

"Yes! You are such a good dog! You're doing Pull, Lacey. Pull! Pull!"

Eventually, it seemed as if Pull meant "let's take a walk and eat treats." Though the trailer was heavy, those treats made it worthwhile.

I didn't have to be told to turn up a particular driveway; we had been there every few days all spring. Wenling jumped off the trailer and used her sticks, and I followed her gamely. She knocked on the front door, and when it was opened, the now familiar white-haired woman stood there, looking puzzled. "What happened to you?"

"I broke my ankle."

"Oh no."

"And I'm so sorry that I'm late with your eggs, but I'm back on schedule. Next time, I'll have your cucumber and tomato plants. It's safe to plant them in your garden now."

"Brilliant," the woman said with a smile. "Thank you so much, Wenling. And thank *you*, Lacey."

I felt approval radiating from the woman. The white dog, whose name I had come to understand was Winnie, had jumped up on a couch and was watching us suspiciously out the window. The woman came over to us and rocked the trailer a little as she picked up something from it, then walked back into her house. Winnie jumped down.

"This is working," Wenling told me.

It was very tiring to pull the trailer with my girl sitting on it, but it was what she wanted to do. We even took the trailer in ZZ's truck to the farm, where Cooper and Burke were waiting for us.

Wenling sat on it. "Pull, Lacey," she told me.

Cooper stared at me. Now Pull meant something to both of us. He gave Burke an offended look. I guess he thought *Pull* was a word only for him, but I was eager to show him that it was my word now, too.

Burke understood. "Good dog, Lacey!" he praised.

Cooper seemed even more insulted by this. Later, though, Burke told him *Okay,* and Wenling unhitched the trailer, and I ran around and around with Cooper. I could tell that he felt better.

I wished Burke would say *Okay* more often.

Later, the people all sat at the table, and Cooper and I took up strategic positions close by. The sound of chewing accompanied the delicious scent of pork wafting through the air.

"Grandma, would you please pass your world-famous biscuits?" Grant requested.

"Gladly," Grandma replied.

"Seems like you're setting a new record tonight, Grant," Chase drawled. "How many is that?"

"Four hundred and nine. I've been counting," Burke answered. Everyone laughed. Cooper's tail twitched into a small wag—when people are in a good mood, treats flow.

"Tell you what, ZZ," Chase said. "We maybe should get started on the orchard before zucchini starts to come in, instead of waiting until July. We'll be working dawn till dusk when that happens."

ZZ nodded wordlessly, and Wenling shot Burke a stricken look. Grant looked back and forth between the two of them, a puzzled frown on his face. I glanced at Cooper, and he felt it, too: something was stirring the emotions of our people.

Something bad.

Later, Burke and Wenling were scraping plates and washing them at the sink. Little bits of pork fell in a steady, delightful rain from those dishes, and Cooper and I were most appreciative. Many dogs will lunge and try to take all the treats for themselves, but Cooper and I have an understanding and we take turns. In our easy, loving relationship, greed would be misplaced.

"Hey," Grant said, stepping into the kitchen. "Need some help?"

"We got this," Burke replied, wheeling a stack of silverware over to Wenling.

Grant leaned against the wall, looking back and forth between my girl and Cooper's boy. "So what's going on?" he asked. "Did you two murder somebody? Because you're sure acting like you've got some big secret."

Wenling shook her head. "No, that's not it."

"Though we were talking about murdering *you*," Burke said. "Except no one would care."

Grant grinned. Then he focused on Wenling. "No, seriously. What's up?"

"It just seems wrong to cut down the orchard for so little money," Burke finally explained.

Wenling nodded emphatically. "The farm's apples and pears are, like, famous."

"Famous?" Grant asked skeptically.

"I'm serious. There's a line for them at your table at the farmers' market. I know that with the mill closed, there aren't any big buyers, but we still make a lot of money at the market."

Grant nodded. "Yeah, but I guess we need the money now, not at the market in the fall. Plus, you know, it's a lot of work to make a few bucks handing over apples one at a time."

"Selling fruit at the farmers' market is part of the soul of the farm," Wenling insisted.

"The soul of the farm," Grant repeated, raising an eyebrow.

"She's right, Grant. Come on," Burke countered. "If we chop down the orchard, it's like cutting off our arms. It's the first step toward dying."

Grant shook his head. "No, the first step toward dying is when you can't pay your bills. Quit being so dramatic."

"Burke and I are saving our money so that our fathers don't have to cut down the trees," Wenling blurted. Burke started in surprise, staring at her. "But if they're going to do it this week," she continued, "we won't have enough."

Grant looked shocked. "You're serious."

Wenling nodded.

"How much money do you two have?"

"Nine hundred and fifty dollars," Wenling responded dismally.

"We're two hundred and fifty short," Burke added bitterly.

There was a long moment of silence.

"You guys are good at keeping a secret," Grant said with admiration in his voice. "I had no idea."

"We had to keep it secret. If my dad really understood how much time it's taking, he'd make me quit. He'd tell me I can't afford to take time from my studies,"

Wenling explained. "But he's wrong. My grades are as good as ever."

"Two hundred and fifty is a lot of money," Grant said. Nobody responded.

"So," Grant continued slowly, "you know that Dad has been letting me go out and work other farms this spring, bring in some extra money."

"Actually, he's doing that because he's hoping someone will adopt you out of this family," Burke replied.

The two brothers grinned at each other momentarily. "Dad lets me keep some of the money," Grant continued. "I mean, I would give it all to him, but he won't take it. Says I deserve to hang on to some because I'm doing the extra work, and that if the farm were just doing better, I could keep all of it."

There was another silence.

"I guess what I'm saying," Grant concluded, "is I've got that. I've got two hundred and fifty."

Burke and Wenling were staring at him.

"I'll be right back," he said casually. Grant left the room, and Cooper and I looked at our people. Something had just happened, something that had switched the mood in the room to part excitement and part what felt like surprise. I wondered if it had to do with the small bite of pork left on the counter that I could smell from where I was standing. I hoped so.

Grant came back into the room and handed something to Wenling. Wenling threw her arms around Grant, and he laughed in shy surprise.

"Thank you! Thank you so much, Grant," Wenling gushed. "This is amazing."

The people all looked at one another.

"I guess now the question is," Burke said, "when do we give them the money?"

"You'd better get it done. Dad pulled the chain saws out this afternoon," Grant told him.

There was a silence. "Tomorrow," Wenling decided. "First thing."

We rode with ZZ back to Cooper's farm the next morning. Wenling left the trailer behind, but of course I still had my cart, and of course when Burke greeted us, he was in his chair. It occurred to me in that moment that Burke and I shared that in common, though he had a dog and I *was* a dog, which I supposed was a pretty big difference.

Wenling and Burke were jumpy and excited as they walked us to the barn. Cooper did Pull, but I did not. It was one of those times when my girl wanted to lean on her big sticks and hop along rather than having me do Pull as she sat on the trailer.

Chase was in there working on a tractor, the same one that Grant often drove. I could see and smell that

Chase's hands were smeared with dirty oil. He was concentrating and didn't look up until we were right in front of him.

"Wenling has something to say to you, Dad," Burke told him.

Chase had a puzzled smile on his face as he wiped his hands on a smelly rag. He raised his eyebrows. "You two look like you're holding your breath."

Wenling and Burke both laughed nervously.

"I've been making really good money selling eggs and seedlings from the hothouse," Wenling finally announced.

"And I've been refereeing basketball, and Grant's getting money from doing farm work," Burke added.

"So we all chipped in. We think it would be a mistake to chop down the orchard and sell it for firewood, so we want you to sell it to us instead." Wenling reached into her pocket and pulled out a crinkly envelope. "That's one thousand two hundred dollars."

Chase's mouth opened in surprise.

"This way, you and ZZ don't need to head up there with chain saws," Burke explained.

"And in the fall, we'll sell fruit at the farmers' market, and I'll add apples and pears to the trailer when Lacey and I make our deliveries," Wenling finished. "Who knows, we might even make a profit. That's how farming goes, right? Sometimes good, sometimes better." She smiled.

Chase reached for the envelope and looked inside. Then he raised his eyes and gave Wenling an easy grin. "This is amazing. You did this, Wenling?"

"We all did. Burke and Grant and me.'

"She did the most work," Burke spoke up. "And Grant said he got paid for working other farms, but I think he probably held up a bank."

Chase was still smiling. "I sure do appreciate this, I really do, but I'll tell you what. Your father wants you to go to college, Wenling, and that's where your share of the money should go. Burke, same for you and Grant. Don't worry too much about what the grown-ups are up to. Like you just said, farming is a business that goes up and down, and this is just one of those bad spells. We've been here through a couple of different generations, and when I'm gone, the farm will still be here."

And just like that, all the happiness went out of my girl and Cooper's boy. We looked at each other in concern. What had happened?

"So you're going to cut down the orchard?" Burke asked.

Chase shrugged. "You've got to do what you've got to do."

16

I could sense that Wenling was very unhappy. Her eyes were lowered as she accepted the envelope back. I sniffed at it and then gazed up into her face. I could understand how she felt. She'd tried to get rid of this papery thing that didn't even smell good to eat, and now Chase was handing it right back to her.

But Wenling didn't look at me. She raised her knuckles to her eyes. "I'll be back in a minute," she muttered. She turned awkwardly on her long sticks and stumped out of the barn toward the house. I started to go after her, but Burke raised a hand. "Stay, Lacey."

Whatever he was saying, it was clear something was

going on and that Wenling had gone away, leaving me here. I hesitated, wondering what to do.

Burke turned and frowned at Chase. "You should say you're sorry and take the money," he scolded. "We've been working on this all year."

Chase shook his head. "I can't. Wouldn't be right, taking money from our own children."

"You take money from Grant."

"I *borrow* money from Grant. I'll pay back every penny when things improve."

"Okay, but you said you needed to sell the trees in the orchard to make money. Twelve hundred dollars, you said. So we raised the money. Sell the trees to us instead, at least for this year's harvest. This is *important*."

Surprised, Chase looked searchingly at Burke.

"I know you think we're just kids," Burke continued, the frustration clear in his voice. "But we want to help. You said it: the farm will be here for generations. That includes us. And we want to sell the fruit in the fall. We love the orchard and don't think you should cut it down unless you're desperate. And if you're desperate, you should take our money. Then in the fall, if we're not able to make anything on the fruit, you can cut the trees down then. But *this is wrong*."

Cooper was gazing at his person because Burke's

voice was so harsh. Chase stiffened. "Mind your tone with me, son," he chided softly.

Burke lowered his eyes.

"The orchard really mean that much to you?" Chase asked. "To Wenling, and even Grant?"

Burke nodded. "Some of my earliest memories are of going to the farmers' market with fresh apples and pears. I was so proud to see our family name on the crates. And maybe with the mill closed, other families will do what you're planning to do and cut down their trees, and then next fall, we'll be the only people who have fruit to sell, and we'll get a better price."

Chase cocked his head. "Guess I didn't think about that, but you make a good point." He scratched his chin, and I notice that his greasy fingers left a black streak there. "I didn't realize all three of you had put this kind of thought into it. ZZ and I just figured you liked to play in the orchard. Climb the trees and such. Come back down the hill and complain to me about the dam spill-way." Chase gave his son a grin.

"We want to give you twelve hundred dollars because we're betting the market will come back," Burke replied simply. "It's business, Dad."

I turned my head sharply because I heard the front door of the house swing open and I smelled my girl. She trudged through the grasses toward us, not meeting my happy gaze. She was coming back! Her shoulders were a

180

bit slumped, but I knew that, since she was returning to her dog at last, I'd be able to cheer her up.

"Wenling," Chase greeted her. "Mind chatting with me a minute?"

Wenling looked up at him. I licked her hand.

"Burke explained what you've been up to. I'm sorry. I was thoughtless."

"The orchard is my favorite place in the world," Wenling told him simply. "But this is about more than that. I really feel that if you cut down the trees, it's the first step to going out of business."

Chase gazed at her for a moment. "What you three have done is a great thing, Wenling. A farm only survives when everyone does their fair share. Here ZZ thought he was doing you a favor by sparing you the hard truth of that, but you three figured it out on your own anyway." He sighed. "They tell me there comes a day when you start learning life lessons from your own children, and I guess that day's come for me. Thank you, Wenling. We'll take your money, and we won't cut down the orchard."

M y girl was happy. It showed in the way she turned her smiling face to the sun and the singsong way she spoke to me as I pulled the trailer to visit people and hand them boxes of egg balls.

I was happy because she was happy. Though the truth is, I was usually happy, no matter what was going on.

We had just returned home from a day of visiting people and giving them tiny amounts of dirt in small cups when my nose told me a big rain was coming. This was not unusual. But I was surprised by the way the wind suddenly blew cool on what had, up until then, been a hot day.

"Come on, Lacey! We don't want to get rained on!" Wenling called from her seat on the trailer behind me.

I felt excited by the energy in her voice, and I pulled a little faster. By the time we made it home and up the ramp, I was panting.

Wenling and I stood by the big window in the living room, looking out. "Wow," Wenling said softly. The sky darkened, and rain fell in a roar. The trees were thrashing, whipped by a wind that shook our house. "It's really coming down!"

I stood next to Wenling as she peered out into the storm. I figured we were spotting for squirrels. Then my ears picked up something in the distance—a long, high howl like an animal addressing the moon. But this wasn't an animal. There was a very machinelike quality to the sound.

Wenling turned her head. She'd heard it, too.

ZZ walked into the room. "Tornado siren." he told Wenling.

Mom joined us, and I could sense that she was worried. "Is that what I think it is?"

ZZ nodded.

Whatever was making that howl, it wasn't getting any closer—it was a steady wail, rising and falling but not growing louder. At times, the wind stole the sound away.

"We should get down to the basement," Mom said firmly.

I blinked as a sudden change overcame the house, a difference in sound and light.

"Oh! There goes the electricity!" Wenling exclaimed.

There was a crack outside, a loud bang, and more wind-driven rain came pouring down. I was surprised when Wenling unfastened the leashes that held me to my cart and ZZ picked me up. His arms were so much bigger than Wenling's! I watched my girl anxiously to make sure she was following us as ZZ carried me down the steps to a place I seldom went. It was called the *basement,* and it was damp and a little dark down there.

"Here," Mom said. A white light came from a toy she held in her hands. Wenling and ZZ both reached into a box, and then they had lights, too. I was the only one without a light-giving toy, but I was just a dog.

ZZ placed me on the floor, which was cool and pleasantly smooth. When the three people with me walked over to sit down on a bench, I followed easily.

Wenling was nervous—I felt it in the tension in her fingers as she stroked my fur. "What happens if a tornado comes?" she wanted to know.

ZZ shook his head. "Not going to happen."

"But if it does," Wenling insisted, "it can rip the roof off." Her eyes grew wide. "The chickens! I need to go get the chickens."

"You're not going anywhere," ZZ replied.

"I'm sure they'll be fine," Mom reassured Wenling. "They're holed up in the henhouse, dry and happy."

I sensed her distress. ZZ and Mom were concerned, as well. The tension made me start panting again.

"Raining hard," ZZ observed.

Wenling sat up straight. "Burke said the next big rain might burst the dam at that old cider mill above the farm."

ZZ and Mom exchanged glances. "Well, let's hope that doesn't happen," ZZ said.

Mom raised her eyebrows. "That's all you have to say?"

ZZ shrugged.

When the lights came back on, I realized I had fallen asleep with my head in Wenling's lap. I had no sense of how long we had been down in the basement, but I knew that it was ZZ who carried me up the stairs. He put me into my cart, and Wenling fastened the leashes.

"We should go make sure the farm is okay," Wenling declared.

ZZ shook his head. "We've got a leak in the ceiling," he noted. "I need to fix that first."

"But, Dad!" Wenling cried out. "What if the dam did fail?"

"Chase can take care of himself," ZZ responded. He turned and left the room, and soon, I heard him using tools to make small noises in one of the bedrooms.

"Mom," Wenling implored. "I'm scared something happened. Can *you* take me?"

Mom gave Wenling a sympathetic smile. "I don't want to overrule your father. And I agree with him— Chase is a very capable man."

"LiMin," ZZ called from down the hall. "The leak dripped on the blanket."

ZZ sometimes says *LiMin* to Mom. I have no idea what it means.

"I'd better go see," Mom told Wenling, turning away.

Wenling sighed as Mom walked out of the room. She limped over to me and petted my head, and then she leaned down.

"We have to go check the farm," she told me urgently.

It was lightly raining outside when we stepped out on

the back porch. I felt the tug as the trailer was hitched to my cart. When we journeyed down the ramp and into the backyard, my front paws squished. The going was a little more difficult because the ground had turned soft.

"Okay, let's go. You can do this, Lacey," Wenling urged me. She led me to the gate, but when we reached the driveway, I heard her set her underarm sticks on the trailer and felt it move as she climbed aboard. "Okay, let's go, Lacey. Let's go. Pull."

Well, this was familiar. I trotted to the end of the driveway and could tell from the way that Wenling was leaning in the trailer that she wanted me to go in the direction that led toward Cooper's farm.

If we were going to go play with Cooper, I was more than willing to pull the trailer some more and even to put up with the wet road under my paws.

We hadn't made it very far in the falling rain before I heard the splashing of a vehicle approaching. The sound soon resolved itself into the familiar notes of ZZ's truck. He pulled alongside, and I halted instinctively.

Mom stepped out of the vehicle. ZZ stayed inside. "Wenling, what are you doing?" Mom demanded.

"I couldn't just sit there. I have to find out what happened."

"I'm sure the phones will be up soon, and then you could just call Burke."

"Please, Mom."

Mom looked at the truck, and ZZ shrugged. Then he got out, too. Wenling climbed out of the trailer, and ZZ put both the trailer and my cart in the back. He lifted me into the seat for a car ride with my girl.

I guessed that ZZ and Mom wanted to go play with Cooper, too.

We followed my nose to the farm. I was surprised to see that Chase had made some major changes! The front part of the house was gone. As we drove up the driveway, I could see right into the living room. And the barn where we sometimes went to watch Burke throw a ball through a hoop had been completely removed. Loose boards lay everywhere in the mud.

"ZZ!" Mom cried urgently.

Alarm and fear crackled off my girl's skin, so I turned my attention to her.

"Stay here," ZZ directed sternly. He and Mom jumped out of the car and dashed up to the farmhouse. "Chase!" ZZ called.

I heard my girl sigh restlessly. She was unhappy. I licked her hand.

ZZ vanished around the back of the house. "They're checking the basement," Wenling told me. She looked around. "I can't just sit here. Come on, Lacey." She eased out of the vehicle, hopping on one foot, and picked me up. She leashed me to my cart and set the trailer behind it and climbed on.

"Let's take a look around," she suggested. "Pull, Lacey."

I went in the direction I was facing, straight toward the wet gash in the dirt where the barn had been. I couldn't really make any sense of what I was seeing— there was just water, broken boards, and a tree lying sideways.

"Their trucks are here. I don't think they left," Wenling murmured. "Where could they be?"

She stood still. I heard birds chattering and the ducks lecturing each other down at the pond, but nothing else. Mom and ZZ were still up at the house.

Wenling looked down at me. "I'm scared, Lacey."

The way she said my name wasn't happy.

Everything was painted with wet, so the odors on the air were all different. I smelled damp wood, mud, and leaves. I also, I realized, smelled Cooper.

He was nearby.

I gazed up at Wenling. Were we here to find Cooper? If so, why didn't Wenling follow his scent, which was coming from someplace close to the tipped-over tree?

I decided that if I could smell my best dog friend, then he could smell me. And I was right. Suddenly, Cooper started barking. It was a strange, muffled bark, as if he were in a car with the windows rolled up. It felt so strange to hear my friend bark but not be able to see him. Even so, I barked back encouragingly.

Immediately, I heard shouting, and it, too, was oddly muted. "Hello? Hello? Help!"

Wenling started in surprise, then turned toward the house.

"Dad!" she screamed.

17

Mom and ZZ ran across the wet grass, their feet
making splashes.

"They're in the storm cellar!" ZZ went to the big tree
and yanked on it.

"Hurry!" came a muffled yell.

"We need to move this tree," ZZ declared grimly.

ZZ ran away. I watched him go, utterly baffled. Why
would he leave when Mom and my girl and me and our
friends were here? Didn't he want to be with us?

He came right back, though, driving his truck. He
leaped to the ground and rolled out some chains that
he wrapped around the tree. Then he backed up his
truck. The tires bit into the mud and threw it in high,
wet splashes.

The large tree that had been lying on its side was slowly pulled away, revealing what looked like a door set in the ground. As soon as the tree was off, Mom reached forward, grabbed the doors, and flung them open.

I was astounded. There were Burke and Grant and Chase and Grandma, all huddled at the top of a set of stone steps. I couldn't see the bottom of the steps, because they went straight down into a pool of muddy water.

Cooper was there, his fur drenched. He'd been able to go swimming. I wondered why he went in what looked like a basement full of water when there was such a nice pond nearby, with ducks to harass.

Chase carried Burke as everyone climbed up out of the ground. They were shivering. Grant was dragging Burke's chair, which leaked water as Chase set Burke in it.

They all stared at the house, then where the barn used to be, then at the house again.

"Why was the cellar full of water?" Mom asked.

It was Burke who answered. "The woodstove down there had a chimney pipe. When the barn blew over, the foundation filled with water, and we couldn't stop the flood from coming down the pipe."

"You could have been *killed*," Mom breathed.

Chase nodded grimly. "It was looking pretty bad.

I don't know how much longer we could have lasted. Thank you for coming, ZZ. You saved us."

ZZ shook his head. "Thank my daughter. She was the one who insisted we come here."

"Thank you, Wenling," everyone said. I liked it when people said her name.

We all piled into trucks and drove to our house. The people who were wet wanted to keep getting wet, so they took turns going into the bathroom and standing with hot water running down on them. Mom did laundry. When everyone was dry, they put on clean clothes and then laughed.

"I don't know who looks more ridiculous in ZZ's clothes, me or Grant." Chase chuckled.

"And Burke's dressed in Wenling's top." Grant said with a snort.

"It's a sweatshirt," Burke said back to him. "Sweatshirts don't have *genders*."

"Give me another forty minutes and you can dress in your own things," Mom told them. She turned to Chase. "How're you doing? It must have been quite a shock to see the damage."

"Well, I was going to have to replace that barn sooner or later," Chase replied with a shrug. "I've got insurance. I guess we'll rebuild. What else am I going to do?" He and ZZ regarded each other. "Give us a nice project for the winter, raise a new barn, don't you think, ZZ?"

I really loved that night because everyone slept in our house. Wenling and Grant and Burke slept in the living room. Burke and Wenling were on separate couches, and Grant was on the floor in the same blankets Wenling had used in the hothouse. Cooper and I pressed against him and each other.

We eventually did a car ride back to Cooper's farm. The water was mostly gone, though the mud smelled fresh and good. I loved seeing Cooper's paws kick it up after he was told, "Okay."

I stuck with Wenling because she was walking with obvious purpose, stumping around with her long sticks. She and Burke were moving about the yard, picking up the dark bottles that were scattered everywhere.

"There's a couple hundred more of those floating in the pond," Chase observed, "and all the way down to the ditch by the road."

"Why the bottles?" ZZ asked.

Chase shrugged. "Must have been stacked up in the cider mill warehouse. When the flood hit, it washed them down here."

"Should we take them back?" Wenling asked.

Chase shook his head. "Nobody there. I haven't been

able to get anyone to answer the phone. They just up and left."

"Could Burke and I have the bottles?"

Chase stared at her in surprise. "Why?" he asked.

"I have an idea," Wenling said simply.

"Well . . ." Chase took off his hat and scratched his head. "I can't think of a reason why not. And your ideas are usually good ones."

Burke and Wenling went back to picking up bottles. "It's not just a good idea," Burke told her. "It's an *awesome* idea."

First it was chickens, then it was bottles. Sometimes my girl just got fascinated with very strange things. I wished she would become fascinated with treats, but she was so focused on those bottles, it sometimes seemed as if she forgot I was there.

Wenling and Burke carefully washed every bottle in a tub next to Cooper's garage, stacking each one in a box. When they had two boxes full, they put them on my trailer and we hauled them up the hill. Wenling was still walking with sticks under her arms. At the top of the hill was the place where all the trees were in rows. It smelled very nice up there, sweet with flowers and a promise of a warm summer to come.

Burke slid out of his chair, telling Cooper, "Assist,"

and made his way to the base of one of the trees. Wenling stood on one leg and held my leash while Burke climbed the tree, pulling himself up with his arms from branch to branch. Slung on his back was a sack with a couple of those bottles tinkling inside of it.

Cooper watched all of this in alarm. I thought I understood his concern. Burke was a boy who sat in a moving chair. Burke was not a boy who would climb up to the treetops. But there he was, hoisting himself up. And there was nothing Cooper could do to help.

"You're as strong as Lacey," Wenling observed.

"Well, yeah, I guess like your dog, I do all my work with just two of my limbs. Man, we've got a lot of bottles."

"We have a lot of fruit trees," Wenling responded.

"That's true. I'm kind of hoping, though, that we finish this before my dad finds out what we're doing. I don't think he'd be happy that I'm climbing trees, especially with what happened to you."

Cooper watched intently as Burke threaded a flower deep into a bottle and tied the bottle into place. "You sure the bottle won't kill off the apples?" he asked Wenling.

"I don't think it will. I can't figure out how else that man at the farmers' market did it."

Every day after that, we took a car ride to Cooper's farm. After several days, as we pulled up in ZZ's truck, Chase was standing in his driveway with his arms folded. Burke was there and Cooper was doing Sit.

"So, Wenling," Chase greeted us as she climbed out and put her sticks under her arms. "Burke says it's a secret that only you can reveal. You want to tell us what you're up to in the orchard? Because I've been up there, and I can't make any sense of it."

ZZ frowned at Wenling as he lifted me out of the truck and put me in my cart.

Wenling was smiling and nodding. "Yes, I'm ready to show you now."

We made our way up the familiar path to where the trees grew in rows. I could hear the gentle creaking and tinkling of the bottles in the trees. I wondered when Burke was going to climb up there and bring the bottles back down. I decided I was ready to cart them around when he did so.

ZZ and Chase looked up into the trees and were silent for several moments. "Well," Chase finally declared. "I got nothing. You've got what looks like a thousand bottles in the trees, like you've decorated for Christmas."

ZZ turned to Wenling. "Explain."

"See," Wenling replied nervously, "when I saw the man selling the apple brandy at the farmers' market with an apple in the bottle, I couldn't figure out how he got the apple in there."

"That's when Wenling got one of her famous ideas," Burke interjected.

Wenling nodded. "Right. Then I realized that an apple blossom would fit through the neck. When the fruit appears, it grows inside the bottle."

Chase glanced at ZZ. "You have any idea she was doing this?"

ZZ shook his head.

"How'd you get the bottles up there?" Chase wanted to know.

"Burke did most of the work because of my leg."

Chase frowned at Burke, who shrugged and grinned. "I'm better at staying in the tree than Wenling."

"Very funny," Wenling said.

Everyone smiled.

"Well," Chase finally drawled, "I guess what we do now is wait for the fruit to grow."

As summer went on, Wenling gave up her sticks and the trailer rides and instead took to walking next to me again. I realized I missed having her back there—it filled me with a special sense of purpose to be pulling her behind me.

But a dog's purpose is whatever a person decides it is.

The weather was turning a bit cool again, and I could tell we were due for another time of rain, dry leaves falling gently from the trees, and then finally snow. On a day when the air smelled fresh and delicious, we drove with ZZ to Cooper's farm, and then ZZ and Chase came with Wenling, Burke, me, Cooper, and a woman who smelled like apples up to the rows of trees.

I noticed that the trees also smelled like apples. Chase pulled down one of the bottles and handed it to the new woman.

"That's so pretty!" the apple woman exclaimed. She raised her head, taking in all the bottles, which were sagging at the end of their branches, heavy with the fruit within.

"We're going to start taking apples and pears to the farmers' market next week," Wenling advised.

"Oh? How much does an apple fetch there these days?" the woman asked. She had very short hair, and she decided to run her hand through it, almost as if she were petting herself.

"Two dollars a pound," Wenling answered promptly.

"Well, two dollars," the short-haired woman repeated, speaking to Chase. "Baby food company is paying a nickel a pound." She gazed at the bottle in her hand. "Tell you what." She fixed ZZ and Chase in a shrewd stare. "I'll go five dollars each for the fruit in a bottle."

Chase shook his head and pointed at Wenling and

Burke. "You need to talk to them. They bought the whole harvest from me back in the spring."

The woman blinked, then looked at Wenling. My girl said, "You can sell your brandy for at least twice as much when there's a whole apple or pear in the bottle."

"That's true," the woman agreed reluctantly.

"We'll harvest them for you, too. There's a trick to getting them out of the tree. You give us boxes, and we'll box them and tractor them down to the driveway for pickup," Burke added.

"Sounds like you two've talked this through already," Chase observed.

"Yes, sir," Wenling replied.

"Ten dollars," the woman grudgingly offered.

"I'm sorry, but the price for the fruit in the bottle is twenty-five dollars each."

The woman stared.

"The man at the farmers' market was getting seventy-five dollars for a quart, and these are half gallon. If you buy them from us at twenty-five dollars apiece, you'll still be making more than double your usual profit," Wenling reasoned.

The woman turned away and peered up into the trees. Then she turned back to Burke and Wenling. "All right, it's a deal."

Everyone was grinning, and Cooper wagged a little.

The short-haired woman reached out to briefly hold Wenling's hand, then Burke's.

The people all looked so happy, I thought they'd be wagging tails if they had them.

"As long as your trucks are going to be here, why don't you buy the rest of the apples and pears to make your brandy with? You have to buy it from somewhere. You'll save money if you pick everything up in one trip," Wenling said.

The woman looked thoughtful.

"Twenty-five cents a pound, and you can have it all. We'll inspect each piece of fruit, too, so you're only getting unbruised, fresh pears and apples."

"Twenty," the woman countered.

"Done," Wenling responded promptly. She grinned.

That night at dinner, everyone was so happy as they ate Grandma's pie. I would have been happy to be eating that pie, too.

Cooper and I paid attention to how our people were feeling, though we were far more focused on the beef that Chase sliced and passed to the people but not the dogs.

"Well, ZZ, you used to own half of nothing, and now you own half of a successful bottle farm," Chase pointed out cheerfully.

"It's good," ZZ affirmed.

"Time to plant more trees in the orchard."

"Yes."

"And," Chase continued, pointing at Wenling, "all because of this one here. Did you see your daughter in action today? She's got to be one of the best salespeople I've ever met. I about fainted when she pushed for twenty-five bucks. I would have taken five."

"She is a good salesperson," ZZ agreed, nodding. "And also . . ."

Everyone watched ZZ expectantly.

"Also . . . a very good farmer."

Everybody cheered then. That's a noise that dogs don't understand, but even Cooper was excited, and when he barked like a regular dog, I barked, too.

Some of that beef made it into our dinners that night, and then Wenling and Burke took a walk with Cooper and me down to the pond. The ducks were huddled on the dock but fled to the reeds to hide when we came near, which was the right way to behave. I reflected that they had better manners than our chickens.

Burke said, "Assist," and slid out of his chair, and he and Wenling sat and talked while the moon rose above us. I lay with Cooper, who drowsily closed his eyes.

I was there with my favorite dog and his boy, and my favorite person, my girl. We were at the pond, my favorite place.

I loved my life.

Reading & Activity Guide To

Lacey's Story

By W. Bruce Cameron

Ages 8–12; Grades 3–7

Synopsis

In *Lacey's Story*, canine narrator Lacey and her beloved owner Wenling's unbreakable bond of love and loyalty holds fast when Lacey suffers a life-altering accident. With help from Wenling's best (human) friend Burke and his devoted dog Cooper, Wenling and Lacey successfully navigate the obstacles Lacey's accident raises. But the human and canine characters in the story must face down other big challenges, too. The farm Burke's father owns, and where Wenling's father works, is in a financial crisis. In spite of their young age and their fathers' resistance to the idea that kids should help solve adult problems, Wenling and Burke take it upon themselves to help save the farm. Without letting their age or other limitations deter them, Wenling and Burke demonstrate how perseverance, grit, and dedication can help them save the people, pets, and places they love.

Reading *Lacey's Story* With Your Children

Pre-Reading Discussion Questions

1. Burke, one of the main (human) characters in *Lacey's Story* has a unique challenge to manage. He has to navigate life in a wheelchair. Throughout the story, we learn about Burke's perspective on this challenge and the strategies and resources he uses to manage it. Do you have a particular or unique challenge to manage in your life, or know a friend or family member who does? Can you reflect on some of the lessons learned, personal strengths developed, or sources of inspiration and support discovered because of these challenges?

2. In *Lacey's Story,* when two sixth-grade best friends (Wenling and Burke) learn that Burke's father's farm might go out of business, they put their heads together to figure out how they can help save the farm. It's not easy to be kids trying to help solve a complicated business problem, but they are determined and willing to work hard. Have you ever helped your family, school, or community solve a big problem? What was the problem? Why was it challenging, or unlikely, for kids to be involved in the problem-solving? Did you help raise money, suggest solutions, or offer moral support?

3. When her dog Lacey (the main canine character,

who is featured in the book's title) is injured, Wenling demonstrates incredible love, patience, and creativity to help Lacey not only heal but thrive. Have you ever helped an injured animal or pet, or read or learned about one, who was nursed back to health by its owner, a vet, or volunteers at an animal shelter? In what ways did you or they help the animal friend in need?

Post-Reading Discussion Questions

1. The characters in this book overcome lots of challenges. Considering the story from the other side of the page, do you think it was a challenge for author W. Bruce Cameron to write a story completely from a pup's perspective? What techniques did he use to make Lacey an effective narrator? Can you think of examples from the text that illustrate how W. Bruce Cameron introduces characters, develops a compelling plot, and explores important themes while staying within the bounds of Lacey's point of view?

2. At the outset of the story, we learn that the farm is in jeopardy. How does this challenge shape the rest of the story and the characters' actions and interactions?

3. Wenling's initial response to the information about the farm being in financial trouble is that she doesn't want to move, that she'd miss her friends

and home. How does she broaden her perspective to consider how the situation impacts people beyond herself—such as her father and his business partner, Chase? Have you ever faced a big change or transition where you had to really think about how it might affect not just you, but other people in your life? Can you describe that experience?

4. Over the course of the story, what do you learn about the relationship between Wenling and her parents? How would you describe her mother's approach to situations versus her father's approach? Can you cite specific examples from the text to illustrate the different ways in which each parent interacts with Wenling?

5. Wenling has a heart-wrenching decision to make after Lacey's accident. She and ZZ have different ideas about whether it's more compassionate to help Lacey recuperate or put her to sleep given the severity of the injuries. Would you have made the same decision that Wenling made? Explain why or why not.

6. What does Lacey's accident reveal about the differences or similarities in how people and dogs might deal with an accident or major change in lifestyle?

7. How does Burke help ZZ and Wenling see the parallels between his own (Burke's) circumstances and Lacey's and change their perspectives on how a per-

son (or animal) can have a full, happy life in spite of limitations?

8. How do Burke and Wenling work together to come up with a plan to help save the farm, and the orchard in particular? (Did you predict how the fruit-in-the-bottle "mystery" at the farmer's market would play a role in their efforts?)

9. What does Wenling learn from her mother's admission that she hates fishing, but makes a point of inviting her husband ZZ to go fishing? ZZ has an incredible work ethic, but it can work both for and against him. Can you think of examples from the text that show each side of this character trait?

10. How is the human friendship between Burke and Wenling different from and similar to the friendship between dog buddies Lacey and Cooper?

11. Throughout the story, Wenling's father, ZZ, can be quite stern with her and he isn't a very demonstrative person—someone who is overly expressive with their affection or feelings. But he does show Wenling how much he loves her in other ways. For example, he builds the cart to help Lacey regain mobility after her accident. Can you think of other examples from the story where ZZ demonstrates his love for his daughter through actions rather than words?

12. Do you think Wenling makes the right decision to

let her father think her "project" in the hothouse is for school? Why or why not?

13. How does Wenling's success and commitment in growing her plants—and her business—and taking care of the chickens and selling their eggs along with her plantings help prove to ZZ that farming might be a good fit for her in spite of his recommendation that she pursue a different career path?

14. How does Wenling breaking her ankle after falling out of a tree in the orchard help Lacey understand that her job, or purpose, is not only to love Wenling unconditionally but also to help her? How does this help Lacey understand the difference between being just a fun-loving dog and a working dog (or striking a balance between both)? How does the situation give Lacey new insight into Cooper's relationship with "his person," Burke?

15. Wenling's father, ZZ, is initially upset by the amount of time and effort Wenling is devoting to her "mission" to help the farm and save the orchard because it takes time away from her schoolwork; and, at first, Burke's father, Chase, doesn't want to accept the money that Wenling, Burke, and his brother Grant offer to help save the farm. How do the young people convince the adults to acknowledge and accept their help?

16. What critical role does Wenling play in helping to

save Burke and his family in the aftermath of flood from the dam breaking?

17. Did *Lacey's Story* give you new perspective on how everyone—human or animal, young or old, with or without extra challenges to overcome—can and does contribute to a cause that is important to all of them?

Post-Reading Activities

Take the story from the page to the pavement with these fun and inspiring activities for the dog lovers in your family.

1. **PUP PAIRS:** Best friends Burke and Wenling work together in *Lacey's Story* to get their dogs Cooper and Lacey to work together. After she injures her back and legs, Lacey needs to use a cart to move without being carried. But the cart keeps tipping over. Burke and Wenling figure out how Cooper can help Lacey learn to keep the cart upright. If you have pet dogs in your family or can partner up with a friend or family member who does, ask your child to brainstorm an activity, trick, or task that requires two dogs working together to accomplish. Together with your child, come up with a teaching, or training, plan. Then work together (as a human team) to put your idea into action and see if you can successfully get the dogs to work as a team, too!

2. **DRAW THE PAW:** In *Lacey's Story*, Lacey always likes to be with "her girl" Wenling. She snuggles on Wenling's bed at night, helps her on delivery runs (with Wenling's eggs and plantings on a trailer attached to Lacey's cart), and joins her on visits to Burke's family's farm. Ask your child to think about a special spot or activity they share or could share with their favorite real (or imaginary) pet dog, or a friend or family member's dog. Invite them to draw a picture of themselves enjoying that place or activity with their pup pal. Encourage them to add plenty of detail and color to bring the scene to life.

Reading *Lacey's Story* in Your Classroom

These Common Core–aligned writing activities may be used in conjunction with the pre- and post-reading discussion questions above.

1. **Point of View.** *Lacey's Story* is told from sweet, spunky, fun-loving Lacey's point of view. She shares her unique dog's-eye view of the characters, places, and events in the story. Lacey has quite a lot of observations about her best dog buddy Cooper in particular. She loves him dearly but is confused when Cooper switches into what it takes Lacey some time to figure out is "working" mode. We hear all about Cooper's personality, priorities,

and activity from Lacey's point of view. What do you think we might learn if Cooper was sharing *his* view of things? Write 2–3 paragraphs from Cooper's point of view. You can address general questions, such as: How would Cooper describe Lacey? How would Cooper describe his relationship with Burke? How would Cooper describe his role as a working dog? Or you can pick a particular event or interaction from the book to write about from Cooper's point of view, such as the sledding outing; a transition from playing with Lacey to helping Burke; or working with Lacey in the pond to show her how to move on land with the cart.

2. **Conquering Challenges.** In a one-page essay, discuss how the concept of overcoming challenges or obstacles is explored throughout *Lacey's Story*. Pick one or several challenging physical, emotional, or financial issues or situations to explore in your essay. (For example, the difficult choices Wenling has to face after Lacey gets injured; Chase and ZZ's conflicted feelings about the farm's future; or how Burke, Wenling, or Lacey handle permanent, or temporary, physical limitations.) Be sure to use examples and details from the text to outline the challenge (or challenges) you are examining; the characters, human or canine, involved; how they come up with a solution or strategy; and

how it helps them to effectively handle or manage the challenge.

3. **Text Type: Opinion Piece.** In *Lacey's Story*, Wenling dreams of being a farmer when she is older. Her father, ZZ, all but insists that his daughter pursue a different path because farming is such difficult, unpredictable work. Throughout the story, ZZ and Wenling try to prove their points to each other. Write a short essay explaining your opinion on who you think makes the stronger case and why. Use information from the text to make your argument in support of ZZ or Wenling. Consider what ZZ says and does to show Wenling how hard farm work is and why he wants a different life for his daughter. And examine how Wenling tries to show her father that she has a talent for farming, the right mindset and work ethic for the job, and that she can apply her intelligence and creativity to farm work just as she does to schoolwork.

4. **Text Type: Narrative.** How might *Lacey's Story* be different if Wenling's mother, LiMin, was the narrator? In the character of LiMin, write a few paragraphs about key characters or a significant event from the story, such as Lacey's accident, Wenling's secret "project" in the hothouse, or how she (LiMin) views the relationship between ZZ and Wenling and sometimes tries to help them better understand each other's actions and intentions. How might the

tone and style of the story be different if it was written from a parent's perspective, instead of a pet's?

5. **Research & Present: Agricultural Awareness.** In *Lacey's Story*, we learn about both the pitfalls and potential in farming, and that owning and operating a successful farm requires expertise in science and business. Do online or library research to learn about an aspect of farming or agriculture that interests you. The National Future Farmers of America (FFA) organization at www.ffa.org might be a good place to start. After you have completed and compiled your research, present what you've learned in a PowerPoint or other multimedia-style presentation.

6. **Research & Present: Get Down to Business.** Sixth graders Wenling and Burke prove that even young kids can find jobs and be entrepreneurs if they put their minds to it. They want to help save the farm their fathers' livelihoods depend on, and their own lives and homes are centered around. And they especially want to raise the money necessary to save their beloved orchard from being chopped down. In *Lacey's Story*, these best friends put their learning and earning together to make a difference *and* a profit. Work in pairs or small groups to brainstorm ideas for businesses you could start if you wanted to raise money for a cause or goal. Research and gather information to put together a business

plan. What product or service will you provide? What is the market (or demand) for that product or service? What materials or resources will you need? How will you advertise your business? Explain and promote your business concept and plan in an oral presentation, supported by visual and written materials, such as business cards, advertisements, or informative pamphlets.

Supports English Language Arts Common Core Writing Standards: W.3.1, 3.2, 3.3, 3.7; W.4.1, 4.2, 4.3; W.5.1, 5.2, 5.3, 5.7; W.6.2, 6.3, 6.7; W.7.2, 7.3, 7.7